Through the Bronze Mirror

Through the Bronze Mirror

Speculative Poems and Stories

Carma Lynn Park

Chicago | Los Angeles

Through the Bronze Mirror

Copyright © 2026 by Carma Lynn Park

All rights reserved.

Published in the United States by Match Factory Editions, 2026

ISBN 978-1-966253-19-8 (hardcover)
ISBN 978-1-966253-20-4 (paperback)
ISBN 978-1-966253-18-1 (ebook)

Library of Congress Control Number: 2025949623

matchfactoryeditions.com

Book layout by RD Morgan

Cover art and design by Gretchen Hasse

Colophon design by Randy Cochran

for Mom and Dad

TABLE OF CONTENTS

Museum Shenwu (Divine Things)

I lean over the bronze mirror,
hair falling forward,
light catching its edges, red-blond
flames around a shadow face—
is this the real me,
burning with divinity?

Festival

I had come in the shuttle with no return ticket. I was disposable. I would do the job, and then whatever happened would happen. My master had no further plans for me. That was all right. I understood. It was business.

I caught the floatbus into the city, pushing in amidst a press of bodies. All the shuttle passengers and the people who had come to meet them piled onto the floater, jostling for seats and shrugging good-naturedly when someone else got there first. A woman carrying a small child struggled up the steps, and several people leaped up and gestured her to their seats. I asked the driver about the fare. He waved the back of his hand and said, "It's Festival. No charge today. By order of the king."

The bus skated on its cushion of air, but the driver liked to take turns fast. No one seemed to mind; they just grabbed onto handrails and leaned. Their faces kept cracking into large white grins, and they talked and laughed. Even those who appeared to be strangers to one another spoke and shared candies and tiny red nuts. I listened to their conversations. This planet spoke a variant of standard Galactic. The biggest challenge was to adjust my translator to a smoother, more liquid cadence.

The woman with the child—it was sitting in her lap playing with the beads at her neck—held out nuts and candies to me. I groped through my memory banks for a suitable phrase. "Thank you, but today I must fast."

"On Festival? What a shame."

As we drew nearer the city, the sun sank lower. The fields on either side were velvety with stubble, the grain stacked into heaps of gold. In the distance gleamed the crystal needle at the summit of the palace. Soon I could make out lower buildings clustering around it. Finally, the bus swept beneath the arch at the edge of the city, wound its way through several twisting streets, and pulled up with a sigh of compressed air and a final jostling of passengers. "We have arrived!"

Darkness was settling over the city, the crystal spire gleaming overhead with its own light, growing brighter as the night grew blacker. Below, lanterns on poles poured out yellow light.

I stepped off the bus, observing the crowds of people strolling in gorgeous robes: jade greens, golds, intense cyans, magentas, and scarlets. A white donkey bearing red panniers clip-clopped down the street. Children dipped their hands into the baskets, then ran giggling back to their parents. "The king gives us candy!"

In the plaza, next to one of the fountains, a man tapped a finger drum to start a rhythm, then sang while onlookers hummed along. A vendor bumped my back. "A thousand pardons!" he said. From the tray slung around his neck he held out a glass holding a molten gold liquid, above which danced a blue flame. "Take it to show no hard feelings, Miss."

"Oh. I—" My voice hesitated. I made an adjustment and tried again. "Thank you. Sir? Where are the king and the prince?"

He squinted toward a dais in the middle of the plaza. "Probably still in the High Tower giving out honors. They'll be here for certain for the fireglows."

A crowd of children had gathered, asking for lava-lava. "Mind you blow out the fire before you drink," he cautioned them.

Cupping the glass in my hand to protect the flame, I walked around the plaza, observing the dais from all angles. I could not drink, but the flame in my hand dipped lower and lower. When it finally flickered and burned out, I frowned with regret—it had been so pretty—and put it into a receptacle that held other empty glasses.

My master had not, of course, told me anything beyond the essentials of my mission. Nothing about a festival, lava-lava, or fireglows. It had not been necessary.

One side of the plaza was lined with booths. From a counter spilled fabrics, heavy satins, and fine silks that ran through my fingers like water. Why had I put out my hand to touch them?

The next booth featured sheets of paper in washes of blue and green fluttering from a line stretched between the poles, with graceful, flowing lettering. A woman sitting cross-legged on a rug tucked dark hair behind her ear. She rose. "The poems are all of my own making." She looked pleased and shy at the same time.

I had been well supplied with general knowledge and technical manuals. But my master had not felt it necessary to expose me to poetry. I was silent, with nothing to say.

"Is this your first Festival?"

"Yes."

"Then you must have a gift."

"No, I…"

She closed her eyes and ran her hand along the papers, not quite touching them. "This is yours." She eased it off its peg and handed it to me.

I thanked her and held out a coin uncertainly, my last one, that my master had given me for the floatbus and that had not been needed.

"No, no. It is a gift to sweeten your first Festival."

Then someone else came up, and she turned to give him her attention.

Pressing the paper to my chest, I took it around the corner to read.

Every life is a river
in which joy leaps.
It braids into all other rivers
and runs to the mother ocean.

Standing behind the canvas flap, I read the words over and over. The planet's tiny orange moon made a low arc, then slipped down again as the words twisted inside me.

My master had patted his sash where his gut pushed it out and said to his manager, "The king is sitting on a royal lode of ore, but he refuses to sell. If there's a power vacuum, I can step in and squeeze things my own way. That's business."

The moon's setting seemed to signal the king to come out, walking stiffly, with a woman in a blue uniform close at his side, hand under his arm to support him. Behind them strode a young man who must be the prince. He was a tall fellow with his hair in a braid down his back, ornamented with beads.

Near the fountain, a man was shouting, "Cheers for the king and prince!" Everyone stood and shouted. A woman lifted up a little girl. I recognized them from the bus.

The king nodded gently, and the prince smiled, laugh lines deepening in his cheeks as he reached out to grasp hands that were offered.

I placed myself in shadow at the end of the line of booths. The night breeze was cool on my cheek sensors.

My master had taken me once to the mines, as a bodyguard. He and the manager took a hovercraft to look over the pits. Equipment took bites out of the earth, grinding and scraping. A bitter smell rose through the air. Workers scrambled among the ore-moving carts, their sinews and tendons carved on lean flesh, hands and faces coated with ash, shoulders shaking with coughs.

My master shook his head and sighed. "You've got to move things along. There's that big shipment scheduled next month for the Belt."

In the cooling night, in shadow, I slipped out my needler. No one saw me. All their attention was on the king, inching toward the dais, then pausing at each step. Finally he reached the top and rested a moment, then raised his hand. Across the square a man swept open a net.

Points of light and whirring noises. The lights grouped together and wheeled up and around, and then the wheel burst apart as luminous pieces split off, skimming over the crowd. Fireglows. They swarmed and wheeled again and burst. The crowd sighed.

The manager had tilted his head in my direction. "Shame about the robot."

"Yes, it'll never survive to make the next shuttle out. They'll catch it sure as a spider catches a fly. Besides, it's getting obsolete. I've got a new model ordered. Be here in a couple of flights."

I took aim, but my hand trembled. *Every life is a river.* I made an adjustment, and my hand steadied. I was an excellent shot. My night-adjusted vision, my internal computer ticking off the distance and required velocity, the vertical angle, my steady hand. *Joy leaps.* My hand twitched as I fired, just a tiny motion, but as soon as the shot went off, I knew it was too high. What was wrong with me? What would my master say? I took aim again, my mind running through all the factors, distance, velocity, angle. Then the king put his hand to his chest and sagged forward.

My modulators carried a thousand conflicting impulses, and I stood bewildered, my arm dangling at my side, the needler slipping from my grasp. The king was pressing his hand to his chest, and his legs were collapsing, and people were rushing up to carry him into the tower. The prince put his hand to one eye, then the other, as he hurried after them, and when I adjusted my vision I saw that he wept.

That night the king died of a heart attack, and the prince became king.

A roboticist might say that the complexity of my design, coupled with my new experiences, resulted in revisions to my programming. I prefer to believe that a poem showed me the right path.

Now I write poems, and sell one occasionally. Enough for my needs. I do not eat and require no shelter. All I really require are paper, inks, a pen, and a coin for the floater. Every week I go to meet the shuttle, and every week I go to the bottom of the ramp, watching the passengers as they disembark, chattering, waving to friends and family. I look for the one that hesitates, the solitary one. Soon it will come.

Then I will take its arm, and we will walk through the town. We'll stop at the fountain, drops tossed by the wind sparkling on our cheeks. Children will run and call with joy like birds. The lava-lava vendor will give us drinks, and we'll each raise a handful of flame. Then I will recite my poem, speaking the words of transformation.

Water, Light, Cormorant

It pulls itself up
onto a log,

raises its beak,
stretches out its wings—

asking to be sent tender fish,
giving thanks for sun on feathers—
praying to the river god.

At the River

The bar's big front windows are open, showing a river so wide the other bank is lost in haze. A white ferry at the landing stage sways with the current. People are sitting on benches; many of them are elderly. Everyone seems a little dazed, staring vacantly, not talking to each other. No one has any luggage.

Inside the bar, the dark wooden walls are hung with plaques:

> *I made it through Purgatory and all I got was this lousy plaque.*
> *All roads lead to the River.*
> *Tavern of the dead.*
> *Today is the first day of the rest of your afterlife.*

Sawdust is scattered on the floor. Just a few people are sitting on mismatched chairs at rough-hewn tables. Like the ferry passengers on benches, most appear dazed. Some of them are having a drink or are nibbling on snacks from wooden bowls.

The bar counter is to the right, a long slab of reddish-brown wood with a jar of pickled eggs at one end, sunlight gleaming off the glass. A mirror reflects rows of colorful bottles and Charon's broad back.

Charon is wiping the counter with a rag that smells fresh and lemony. Judging by his looks, he could be young or middle-aged. He is a few inches over six feet tall, with heavy arms and curly black hair. He wears a blue shirt embroidered with red and white thread.

John is the only one sitting at the counter. He is in his 30s, with a baby face and a few gray hairs that don't show among the blond. He's wearing a white t-shirt and is drinking a Hamm's beer, tipping up the bottle.

Charon glances at the clock on the wall. Together, he and John say, "Nearly time for the 2 o'clock."

Charon finishes wiping the counter and sets out a few wooden bowls of snacks. John reaches over, pulls out a potato chip, swivels on the stool to look out the window. "There's a good crowd."

Charon asks, "You crossing today?"

"I'm not crossing today or any day. I'm never crossing. I like it here."

"Not much going on. It's pretty much the same, day after day. People come and they go."

"I like hanging out, having a beer, talking to people coming through. Talking to you."

"That's what Dave said. And he finally crossed."

"I'm sorry he's gone. He made me laugh."

Charon gets a faraway look in his eyes. "His tribe used to get up the morning of a battle and say it was a good day—a good day for dying. They also said that a boy must become a man and take a man's responsibility. That means…"

John grins. "I never heard him say that. I think you're making it up." The grin fades as he tilts his head at a woman alone at a corner table, black eye make-up smeared, a seam in her blouse gaping open under her arm. She stares at the table, muttering to herself. There is a bottle of whiskey in front of her and a shot glass and a bowl of green olives. From time to time she pours whiskey into the shot glass and gulps it.

John goes on, "Neela's the one who should cross over. She disturbs the other customers."

"I think you're the one she disturbs."

Leaning forward and lowering his voice, John says, "She keeps coming in and acting crazy, and after a few days she throws herself into the river, so we get a little peace and quiet. Then she comes back and the whole thing starts over again. I'm surprised the Dark Wood lets her out."

"She can't forgive herself."

"What's her story, anyway?"

"It's hers to tell you, if she will."

Neela slumps over the table, forehead coming to rest on her forearms. The shot glass falls with a thud and rolls on the floor.

Charon puts a sign on the counter. *Sorry, the bar is closed. Go ahead and complain to the higher power.*

Flicking the sign with a finger, John says, "Hey, you'd think after all this time I could tend bar while you're piloting the ferry."

Charon pauses, shrugs, puts the sign away under the counter.

John is startled. "Really? You're finally letting me tend the bar?"

"Don't do anything I wouldn't do."

"Thanks for the car keys… Dad."

As Charon booms out, "Boarding the 2 o'clock. Boarding," John gets up, lifts the flap, and walks around to the other side of the bar.

Almost all of the people in the bar get up and follow Charon. Neela just sits with her head on her arms. A man with white, flyaway hair leans back in his chair and continues to play Solitaire, laying out limp, worn cards.

A small boy jumps up and waves his extended arm back and forth, then charges at John. "Ka-ting! Take that, Captain Hook!"

"En garde!" John curves his hand into the semblance of a hook, and they pretend to fight. The ferry blasts its horn.

John says, "Hey, Peter Pan, you beat me. Now get out of here. You're wanted on the other side." The boy runs off. John says to himself, "Poor little tyke. I wonder what happened to him. Cancer? Accident? I hope the Dark Wood wasn't too hard on him."

He slaps the counter. For a few minutes he busies himself walking around the tables, picking up the glasses and bowls and washing them.

The man with the flyaway hair beckons. John says, "Hey Benjy, how are things going? Another old-fashioned?" He checks the bowl. "Looks like you're okay on the peanuts." He goes and mixes the drink, comes back, and sets it on the table.

"Thanks," Benjy says, taking a sip. "None of those sissy foofy drinks for me, the pink martinis and whatnot. I always used to tell my wife I didn't know how I married a girl that liked sloe gin fizzes. She used to get so steamed up." A smirk creeps across his face. "She'd tell me, 'You've said that a thousand times. It's not funny anymore.'"

"You still waiting for her?"

"Yep. It wouldn't feel right, crossing without her. We were married more than 60 years. That's commitment. Or pigheadedness, not sure which."

John leans one hip against a table. "I was dating a girl. She was cute. Fun. We might have gotten married. Then I went and wrapped my car around a telephone pole."

"Anyone else hurt?"

"Just me. And the car. She was a beauty. 1959 Ford T-bird. 300 HP, V-8, manual transmission. Turquoise with a white soft top. I spent my last cent on her, buying her in payments from Mr. Morton. Cathy used to say I spent all my time tinkering on that car. Spent more time with the car than with her."

"Do you wish you'd married her?"

"She said that's what people did, get married, settle down. But I don't know. She sat at this same table a while back, and I didn't recognize her. She was older, gray in her hair, but still. Charon made her a tequila sunrise, I brought it over to her, and she did a double take, asked if it was me. We talked about some of the crazy things we'd done in our younger days. She told me she'd married my buddy Mike. No kids. She caught me up on what had happened to our friends, the ones she'd stayed in touch with. Then it seemed like we didn't have anything else to say to each other. She took the next ferry across."

The old man takes out a handkerchief, wipes his face. "You have to love the other person so much. You have to love them even when they're lying beside you farting under the covers."

From behind, Neela grabs a fistful of John's t-shirt. He jumps. She speaks in a low, hoarse voice. "I just wanted to go out and have a little fun, that's all. I was so tired of being cooped up in the house. You understand, don't you?"

A man staggers in, head bowed, both hands clutching matted black hair, and collapses on a barstool.

"Customer." With a sigh of relief John escapes from Neela. He returns to the counter, asks the man, "Looks like you need something to take the edge off the Dark Wood. What'll you have?"

Still gripping his hair, the man looks up, mumbles something.

"Sorry, man, didn't catch it. Unlike Charon, I don't speak all the languages of the world." He points to a tap. "Beer?" Points to bottles. "Whiskey? Gin?"

The man shakes his head no, no, no, hunched over, fingers clenching and unclenching in his hair.

John slides a bowl of snacks down the counter to him and makes a face. "They look like little brown crackers wrapped in seaweed. Smell like iodine. You're going to love them."

Neela moans, stumbles out the door.

John calls after her, "Don't walk by the river." Shrugs. "I don't know why I bother. It's none of my business."

The door creaks open. A girl maybe 10 years old, wearing a sari and clasping a white dog to her chest, hesitates in the doorway. "May I wait here? With Pansy?"

"Sure. Next ferry is at 6 o'clock. Can I get you a Coke? 7-Up?"

"I don't seem to have any money."

"It doesn't matter. Everything's on the house." There's a sign on the counter that says *Your money is no good here* and shows a drawing of a dollar bill with Benjamin Franklin putting bunny ears behind George Washington's head.

The girl sits at a table, settling the dog in her lap. "Might I have a lassi?"

"Coming right up." He has to search a bit behind the counter. "Where the heck? Oh, it's in the fridge." He pours it into a glass and sticks a straw in it, brings it over to her along with two wooden bowls. "Here you are." He puts one bowl on the table, looks inside. "Enjoy your candy." He leans over to put the other bowl on the floor. The dog jumps down, shoves her tiny muzzle into the bowl, and begins to crunch. John pats her on the head. "I always wanted a dog, but it's a lot of work."

Benjy asks the girl, "You got a coin for the ferryman?"

Sipping the lassi, the girl nods her head yes, swallows. "I have one for me, but not for Pansy. I won't cross the river without her. We go everywhere together. I was so glad she came with me on this trip. In the Dark Wood, especially, I was quite frightened."

Benjy offers, "She can have one of mine. The wife gave me two, one for each eye." He appeals to John, "But I only need one, isn't that right?"

"That's right."

Benjy and the girl continue talking, but John rushes to the window, leans out, and shouts, "If you fall in and it sweeps you away, you have to live your whole life over—every year, every week, every hour, every minute! I know it. I know you know it." He withdraws his head, then leans out again. "And then you have to go back through the Dark Wood." He walks to the counter shaking his head. "Crazy old bag."

The girl asks the old man, "What's on the other side of the river?"

"I don't know." Again he appeals to John. "You've been here a lot longer than me. Do you know?"

"I haven't been there. Once you cross, you can't come back. Except for Charon, of course, he's the ferryman. Once I asked him, and he said this side is the chrysalis, and the other side is the butterfly. I asked what the heck that meant, and he thought for a minute and just said this side is the bud and the other side is the bloom. I gave up."

A woman walks in the door. Her hair is short and squiggly, and the silver in the black catches the light, seeming to sparkle. She has a big cheerful smile and round, smooth brown cheeks. "Hello, everybody!" The words come out warm, with rich vowel sounds.

John gestures at the room. "Come on in and sit anywhere."

"Thank you." Her rubber flip-flops slap the floor as she walks to a stool at the counter. She gathers up her faded print skirt to slide onto it. "This isn't what I expected. Not that I really thought about it."

John nods as he walks back behind the counter, running a hand over the wood. "I know. You get an idea in your head. Not what I expected either, but it's friendly. I feel at home here."

"It's, um," she searches for a word, "cozy. Not too posh for the likes of me." She nods in a friendly way to the black-haired man and speaks to him slowly and carefully in another language.

The man stares at her for a moment, unclenches his fingers from his hair, then gives a hoarse ha! He shakes his head, says ha! again, and takes a cracker from the bowl.

The woman says, "I thought I was saying hello and asking about his health, but I expect it came out totally different, maybe 'Let us eat radishes in the moonlight.' At least he got a chuckle out of it. I've done a good deed."

John wipes the counter in front of her. "Would you like a glass of wine? A martini?"

"What do you have on tap? Oh, what the hell, whoops! No pun intended—I'm going to treat myself. Do you have Red Kay Ale in a bottle?"

"I never heard of it, but we always—well, here it is." He pops off the top, pours some into a frosty mug, and sets the bottle and mug in front of her.

"Thanks! Oh, I see that the drink is free"—she points at the plaque—"but I don't have any money for a tip. I have the coin for the ferryman. You can have that." She lays a thin silver coin on the counter.

John taps a plaque that says *Please! Do not tip the bartender* and shows a cartoon of a man tilted to one side. "We're not allowed to accept tips." He pushes the coin back to her. "How was your trip?"

The woman gulps some beer. "Ahhh." She wipes foam off her upper lip. "It could have been worse. The whole thing didn't last long. I didn't have to linger and suffer, like my friend Annie. She had cancer. So sad. I don't suppose you remember her coming through? She was petite, red-haired, quiet. Not like me. Annie used to tease me, 'A roaring lion kills no game.' "

"Sorry. I've seen a lot of people come and go." He pauses his wiping. "So what happened?"

"I was speaking at a rally in a park. It was a beautiful day, blue sky, perfect temperature. Usually, I'm not an exciting public speaker, but the words were just marching out of my mouth. 'We will hope, we will pray, and we will do.' The people all turned their heads toward the platform to listen. There was a thud in my shoulder and a noise. Then another thud in my middle," she pats her thick waistline. "It was like being ripped apart. At first it didn't hurt, and then it did. I struggled to breathe, couldn't catch my breath. Then I was… gone." She gulps more beer, looks around.

"Are you looking for Annie?"

"Oh, it's been a long time. No, I'm looking for the man who killed me. Very tall, slender, young? I think Security shot him, although it was confusing, and things happened so fast."

"He won't show up for a while. The Dark Wood will give him a good working over."

"The Dark Wood? You mean that prettyish grove of trees?"

John shivers. "The Dark Wood—a grove of trees." To the woman he says, "You want me to give him a message?"

"Tell him he did wrong, no doubt about it—but I understand being passionate about a cause, and I'm all right now. I just worry about the country until everything gets settled. The factions are…"

John hastily slides a bowl down the counter to her, interrupting the flow of words.

She picks it up, looks inside. "Sesame sticks! This is my lucky day!"

Neela stumbles inside, mud on her shoes. She plops down at her table in the corner, smacks the top with the palm of her hand and mutters, staring straight in front of her.

"You want something to drink, Neela?"

"She looks up for a moment, then goes back to staring and muttering.

John pours a glass of water and takes it over. She begins to cry, mascara streaking her face.

Charon walks in, and John looks up. "Hey, big guy."

"How did it go?"

"Smooth as glass."

Charon says something to the black-haired man in a rapid language with soft consonants, and then he bows. The man stands, answers, and bows low.

Neela's voice is tight. "I didn't know. I didn't know she could climb out of the crib." She runs out of the bar.

Charon greets the woman on the barstool. "Dear lady, I meet you at last. But you're taken too soon from your country."

"I was assassinated."

He clasps one of her hands in both of his. "You gave it your lifeblood."

John points at the door. "Don't you think you should check on Neela? She's been worse than usual this afternoon."

"I'm not allowed to interfere."

John leans out of the window. "Stay away from the river, Neela! I mean it."

Charon is still talking to the woman. "Your grave will be loved."

"Neela! Hold on!" To Charon, "She fell into the river, but she grabbed a tree branch. You've got to do something."

"It's really none of my business." Charon doesn't move.

John looks out the window, back at Charon, out the window again. "Hold on! Don't let go!" He runs out the door and down the dirt path alongside the river, then down the bank, waving his arms for balance. He stumbles, falls, gets up, keeps going.

Neela's arms are wrapped around a tree branch. Water flows across her chin. John wades into the river. The cold current pushes and tugs at him. His knees buckle. He almost goes under but plants his feet. Reaches out a hand. Neela looks at the hand, at his face. Her own face contorts. She lets go. The current pulls her out of sight.

Something bright descends, picks up John and cradles him, and rises into the air. It lets him down gently just outside the door and flies away over the river. He staggers inside and collapses on the floor, dripping water. "I didn't save her."

Charon says, "She has to save herself. Maybe next time."

John scrubs his face with his hands and gets to his feet. "I think I'm ready to cross. Do you have a seat on the 6 o'clock?"

Sky Man / Earth Woman

Sky Man, half blue, half black,
shining skin, cloud-pale eyes,
fingers arching like rainbows.

Earth Woman, opening her womb to the rain,
belly round as the moon,
soles of her feet furry with roots.

All of us –
fur people, people who open and close their shells,
the ones who wear scaled armor shining on the outside,
people who unzip a ghost-skin
to emerge clean and bright,
those who hang by their feet to sleep,
people who wiggle boneless fingers in the tides,
naked-skin people,

we are all of us
their children.

Wider and Deeper

The sorcerer was young, still with a downy beard, his power small and flickering. He set his mind to obtaining greater strength, and after much study he decided to lure the creature of living darkness, whose energies he could then tap. The creature would need a pit, deeper than the lowest basement of his castle, deeper than the copper mines of the Frostshadow Mountain, deeper than the Everquiet Caves. Because blood and fear would stoke the creature's life force and swell its energies, supplying it with victims would give him even greater power.

His mouth stretched in a smile as a plan struck him, and he congratulated himself on his cleverness.

The first step was to capture a quiet, modest animal that snuffled among the leaves on the forest floor. He carved its incisors to chisel the earth, widened its paws to shovel the loosened dirt, and thickened its shoulders with muscle. He modified as many of the animals as he could trap and set them to work. They dented the earth, eating tree roots as they went. The sorcerer forced them to go deeper, and hunger led them to eat beetles and worms and other crawling things. Deeper, below the organic layer. Many starved and died until some were born that could subsist on moist, crumbling dirt. They even came to like it; each layer touched the tongue with its own mineral tang. They gnawed stones, each of which had a texture smooth or grainy, a taste sweet or salt.

Wider, deeper. They learned to work together to dig into the earth and to haul the clumps away. Squeaks and grunts shaded into utterances with complexities of sound and meaning.

The pit dived so deep that no light fingered the bottom, and the living darkness prowled in. The sorcerer felt the dark's power rise within him, and his mouth stretched into a grimacing smile, his teeth black and rotting, his beard scraping his collarbones.

The living darkness hunted the diggers, melted their flesh, and slurped their blood, breaking bones to lick up the marrow. It gorged and grew.

Fear entered the tales the diggers told before sleeping. The sorcerer's power flared within him, and he rejoiced in it, smiting one land after another with lightning and fire, bringing them under his fist.

Eventually, he returned to the pit and ordered the digging to stop. But digging was what the diggers were made for—diggers dig, each generation told the next—and they continued their delving into the earth. No matter, he thought. What harm could it do him?

They learned that the bits of glowing stone they found in the earth made the creature cringe before them. At first they merely warded it away, but as they grew bolder they hunted it until it became shy and slunk through old, abandoned tunnels, whimpering.

The sorcerer's power roiled within his stomach and burnt his bones; his skin felt eaten by acid. All of his remedies failed, and he didn't know why.

Deeper and wider. The pit—now an abyss—ate away at the mountain on which the sorcerer's castle was perched, and from time to time the castle quivered, with a clinking of glass phials and a tinkling of delicate brass instruments.

At last the castle tilted and slid and fell over the edge of the abyss. Tumbling end over end, glass breaking, ancient tapestries streaming out the windows, and chairs and tables of rare and fragrant woods battering against the walls. The sorcerer tumbled in his bed. He clung to the headboard, vomiting clots of blood that clung to his robes and skin and matted his hair. As the castle neared the bottom of the pit, the diggers fled from the screaming of its passage.

It smashed. Walls crashed down. Chunks of broken stone rolled and came to a stop. Then silence. In time, a few brave diggers came back and began exploring the ruins. They edged into the sorcerer's bedroom and found a body sprawled on the bed, misshapen, with long, skinny legs and arms and on its face a mass of something that felt like tree roots. A digger nibbled on the beard, but it tasted bad, and she spat it out. The hideous figure never moved.

They left it and went on to other rooms of the castle, enjoying the tastes and textures of the smoky stone and spicy wood splinters, rolling in silk and wool tatters. One began to sing a hymn of praise and gratitude, and the others joined in.

Crow Eats Carrion

Crow's wife turns up her nose
and turns her back. *You born in a barn?*
He brings her the wishbone of a wren.
Here, sweetie, we'll make a wish
never to be parted.

Oh, you. She strokes the feathers
on top of his head.

When Crow eats carrion
he takes in that animal,
the light step of the deer,
the trembling of the rabbit,
the fish smoothed and smoothed by water.
He thinks he is god.
He stuffs himself.
His stomach hurts. He has a headache.
I'll never do this again.

His wife has a cough that won't go away.
One morning she has blood on her beak.
One morning she doesn't wake,
though Crow calls and calls.
Now he knows for sure he's not god.

He eyes the sleek breast,
the muscle bunched in the thigh,
and knows what to do.
Bending his head,
he begins to nibble on a wing.

A Change in the Weather

Staring out the door to the balcony, John said, "Gray clouds. Gray sky. Feels like forever since we've had sun."

Sarah turned a page of her book, but the corners of her mouth quirked up. "I hid it." She closed the book. "A cat would sit in your lap and purr and cheer you up."

"Nasty beasts. Slinking around. And where would you put the litterbox in a condo? Stink up the whole place. Give it a rest. Forty years, and you still want a damn cat."

"Forty-three years," she said softly.

His shoulders slumped. "I'm just feeling edgy."

That night John shuffled to the bathroom to brush his teeth. Through the closed door he heard his wife muttering, although he couldn't make out the words. He opened the door, and she froze, standing in front of the sink, tracing a design on the mirror with her finger.

John stopped, hand on the door frame. "What are you doing?"

"Peeing before bed. But someone came in and interrupted me." Sarah gave a half-smile.

"Hardy-har. What are those lines on the mirror? Whiskers?"

She leaned toward the mirror, tilted her head. "Is that a new wrinkle on my cheek?"

"You're not as young as you used to be. Anyway, I want to brush my teeth."

Stepping back, she gestured at the sink. "Make yourself at home."

John couldn't sleep. He'd get drowsy, then wake up. Get out of bed, go to the living room to read, go back to bed, get up again.

The next few days were the same. He thought he saw movement out of the corner of his eye, but when he turned his head nothing was there. His thoughts slowed to sludge, pondering the same thing for minutes on end. How long had the sun been gone? It had started—when had it started?

One night when he couldn't sleep, he went out onto the balcony, hoping to get some fresh air. Clouds covered the moon and stars. From 10 floors up it was a long way down to the concrete. His slippers soaked through in the snow.

John crawled back into bed.

"Ugh!" Sarah shivered. "You're damp and cold."

"You're the one who's cold," he muttered. But he rolled over onto his side and huddled into himself.

The next evening Sarah made his favorite—pot roast with onions, carrots, and potatoes, and a green salad on the side. He stared out the balcony window, bleary-eyed, twitching the blinds. "It's been weeks. Where did you hide the damn sun?"

"They say it's a record."

John plodded into the kitchen.

On the counter were olive oil and vinegar for a homemade salad dressing. Sarah got some dried leaves out of an unmarked jar.

"What are those? They smell sort of strange."

"Oh, you know. Eye of newt, toe of frog." She paused, holding the leaves. "Speaking of animals, you know, I'd really like a cat."

He slapped his hand on the counter. "I'm tired of talking about cats. They're all soft, smiling with that upturned cat mouth, then the claws shoot out."

Sarah crumbled the leaves between her fingers and sprinkled them into the salad dressing, stirred it.

They sat down at the table, and he took a hearty helping of the pot roast. "Smells good."

She poured more salad dressing into his bowl.

Sometime that night he went over the balcony railing. A neighbor found the body when she went out for a walk. She called 911, then went to notify the wife—the widow. The younger woman was kind, making tea, rubbing the older woman's back as she sobbed.

The paramedics explained they had to notify the police in the case of a sudden death. They took the body away.

Later that morning, after the neighbor had left to go to work, an officer arrived. He apologized for bothering her and took a statement. "You say he had been depressed?"

"Yes, terribly depressed, and he had bad insomnia. He used to go out onto the balcony in the middle of the night." She patted her eyes with a damp tissue.

"Was he taking anything?"

"I'm not sure." Her voice caught, and she cleared her throat. "He bought some sort of herbal supplement."

The officer nodded. "I don't think I'll need to contact you again. Thank you for your help at this difficult time. My condolences for your loss."

He stood up, glanced out the balcony door. "Sun's finally out."

Sarah watched him walk down the hall, gave a teary nod as he stepped onto the elevator. The bell dinged, and the door closed.

She went back into the condo and took a deep breath, then stopped to wipe her eyes. Punched in the number she knew by heart. "Hello. I want to adopt a cat."

The fa Liri Line

The tea tasting was going well, thought Lady Ilane. The wives of her husband's business associates had all accepted her invitation and were strolling around the club's private room holding tiny translucent cups of jade-cloud tea. Their giggling and gossiping rose over the rustle of heavy silk dresses and the jingling of ankle bracelet chains.

One was confiding, "When I was a girl, the first maid I had ran off with a spacer and never came back. Eventually her mother died, and her father had to go to an elder care facility because there was no one to take him in."

The other nodded wisely. "It comes of having common blood."

Now the waiter offered his tray of black tea with an orange scent. The ladies murmured appreciatively. Engineers had not been able to adapt orange trees to the harsh winters and thin air, and only a few plants grew in the conservatory; the crop was sold at high prices.

Ilane paused at various groups to nod and smile and then move on. A woman was standing by herself gazing at the garden outside where snow whitened clumps of green needles on the pine tree. As she walked over, Ilane thought quickly for the woman's name. Lady Tessamira, from an estate in the country. That explained her dress, which was of good silk but cut in an outdated style. Lady Tessamira swayed, one hand going to the mound of her belly. Ilane moved toward her as quickly as she could, hampered by the chain between the ankle cuffs that shortened her steps. Putting a hand under the woman's elbow, she helped her to a chair.

"Thank you!" The voice was faint. Ilane glanced at the latticework screen behind which the maids were sitting and chattering, their teacups clinking. "May I get your maid, Lady Tessamira?"

"Oh no! I'll be fine when I've rested a little."

Ilane smiled, remembering. "It was just so when I was carrying my son. There were times when I was quite ill. But everything is worth it when you hold your child in your arms."

The Dowager Duchess hobbled over. "Pastries going around with the moonflower tea? It wouldn't have been done when I was a girl." But she didn't hesitate to shoot out a clawlike hand and grab a tart piled with cream.

The duchess went on, "It's a shame what happened at the genetics lab. Your son doesn't have any fa Liri in him, does he, Lady Ilane?"

Taken by surprise, Ilane stammered, "The—the genetics counselor advised it." She and her husband had been so excited to plan their son. They had sat in the counselor's office, inspecting charts with genetic lines that traced colors like neon lights. Yellow for the fa Liri line; it had looked like summer sunshine.

With a protective instinct she schooled her face to smoothness and added, "But my husband will know the details, of course." She sipped her tea, not tasting it. "Is there a problem at the lab?"

The duchess clicked her tongue. "My nephew told me this morning. They found that one of the technicians had substituted his own genes for a batch of the fa Liri genes, then destroyed a lot of the records." Her mouth worked as if she wanted to spit. "Vials of poison. Luckily, he was hired just seven or eight years ago, so the children can't have bred."

The other ladies clustered around. "But how was it discovered?"

"A girl wasn't turning out the way the parents had expected, and at first, you know, everyone thought they were imagining things, but they insisted on getting her tested, and the bad genes were found. The lab tried to keep it quiet, but Enforcement knows its duty. The lab head has committed suicide. The technician will be executed tomorrow."

"Why would anyone do such a thing?"

"It's a clear case of resentment against his betters."

Lady Tessamira stroked her belly. "Thank heavens we never even considered fa Liri splicing."

A waiter offered glasses of iced tea with mint. Ilane's lips felt stiff, but she forced herself to say, "Please, try this tea. It's quite refreshing."

She heard hardly any more of the conversations but forced herself to respond with appropriate, if rote, replies. One of the ladies even told her she was a good listener. All the while she had to force her eyes away from the corner where a clock told the hours, minutes, and seconds.

Finally, one by one, the ladies began putting on their furs, thanking her for the teas and taking their leave. Lady Coco said, "The shops have some new fabrics from the trading ship. Lady Ayala and I are going shopping. Would you like to join us?"

Ilane could think only of hurrying home. "Thank you, no. I cannot today."

Lady Ayala opened her fan and said behind it, "She's going home to read."

Good-naturedly, Lady Coco said, "Sometimes I like to read."

When everyone had gone with a last jingle of ankle chains, maids trotting behind, the proprietor appeared and bowed deeply. Ilane made a point of being gracious to the lower classes, so she thanked him. "Everything went smoothly. The ladies seemed to enjoy it."

"It is always a pleasure to serve you, my lady."

Her maid helped her with her furs, and they went into the cold passageway, the sun glaring off the snow outside. The slidewalk took them to Center Dome, where they passed through the airlock. Through Center Dome to Dome 5, down the walkway lined with trees, and to her own home at last. She pushed the button, and the door opened, letting out a rush of warm air.

Her son ran up. "Mama! Mama!" She hugged him hard, feeling his round head against her stomach.

"Have you been a good boy today?"

Nanny, panting up the stairs from the nursery, said, "He's been playing with that son of the cook next door. I told him he mustn't associate with the likes of that."

The boy looked down, eyelashes dark velvet on his cheeks. "I'm sorry, Mama."

Nanny exclaimed, "Oh, the master wants to see you. Right away, he says."

The maid hung up the furs and asked, "My lady, may I remove your ankle bracelets?"

"No, I must not keep my husband waiting." She stumbled down the hallway with its straw matting, past the watercolors hanging on the walls.

At the closed office door she spoke into the microphone, "Your wife begs to see you."

The door was sucked into the wall. Her husband stood up behind his desk, papers stacked neatly in front of him. She stepped forward with her eyes politely downcast, and he gestured toward one of the leather chairs. Perching on the edge, she folded her hands in her lap.

The electronic gate to the safe in the wall was off, the cavity showing stacks of currency and flat cases containing her more expensive jewels, along with fireproof metal boxes containing their important papers.

Seals and holograms dotting the thick, cream-colored papers on the desk indicated they were official documents. She leaned forward and saw pictures of chromosomes in blues, yellows, greens, reds, pinks, and blacks along with lists of technical terms: …splicing at B197… the composite dexter…

Her husband smoothed his hair, first one side, then the other. "A general bulletin has been issued. About the genetics engineering lab." He paused, and Ilane clamped her lips together. He would tell it in his own way.

He tapped the papers without looking at her. "A technician banked his own genes for batches of the fa Liri genes, and Robbie received some."

All the calls they had gotten from the lab, saying that another set of splicings had failed. That was to be expected, because of the process's difficulty. Then there was one where the cells began to divide, and a blastocyst had grown. When it got big enough, it was implanted. And she had miscarried. She hadn't known she could mourn so much. Three miscarriages before Robbie.

"But there must be some mistake."

"No. Everything is here in these papers. Lines and sublines, batch numbers, splicing points."

It felt like something was stuck in her throat. "What will they do with him?"

"The children will not be mistreated, but they must be segregated. For now, they will be put in Dome 9, where there is an unused barracks. There hasn't been time to arrange the details."

"But he's just a child. He needs his home." Pictures welled up in her mind. A cold barracks with bad food, older children bullying littler ones, a boy crying for his mama. Tattoos on foreheads for identification, as if the children were criminals. Sterilization so they couldn't breed.

She clasped her hands. "The duchess said records had been destroyed. Maybe if we don't tell anyone…"

He reached toward the televisor.

"But he's your son. How can you want to do this?"

"It is not a matter of what I want. It is a matter of honor, of doing what is right."

"Not tonight, please! Just a little more happy time for him."

He hesitated, then said gently, "But I will have to call in the morning."

She pressed her hands to her face.

A desk drawer slid open and closed. The chair rolled back. His footsteps came around the desk. Ilane looked up. He was holding a glass vial in his hand. "I knew you would be upset, so I had the doctor bring something to calm you. Take one." He gave her the vial.

A clear head was needed if she were to help Robbie, but her husband was watching her. "Take it."

She pretended to put a tablet under her tongue but let it fall back into her hand. She drew a breath and exhaled to calm herself. "I'm sorry. May I make you some tea?"

"That would please me."

She moved to the table with its tea service, and her hand hovered over the canisters. Hardly knowing what she was about to do, she said, "I will make you the Smoke Mountain tea. It has a slightly bitter taste, to show my bitterness that I have displeased you." She set out a porcelain cup and measured a scoop of tea into it. Then she poured hot water from the electric teapot. Keeping her back to the desk, she dropped in a couple of pills, wondered if it was enough, then dropped in three more. Taking up the whisk, she began to beat the tea. Her husband was slowly leafing through the documents, eyes somber and frowning, lines carved from nose to mouth. With two hands she offered him his cup.

He took it and sipped. "Bitter indeed." His glance went to the papers. "But fitting."

She knelt on the cushion in front of the desk. After a few minutes her husband began to yawn and put the cup down. She waited, barely daring to breathe. He slumped over the desk, then his head descended to the desktop. She dared to touch his shoulder. "My husband?" He gave a mutter and a snore.

Going to the safe, she put sheaves of currency into pockets sewn in the sash wrapped around her waist. Opening the cases, she stuffed necklaces, rings, bracelets and brooches into her embroidered bag. It hung at her waist heavy and bulging.

The sight of her tense, white face in a mirror brought an exclamation, and she patted her cheeks to get color into them before calling Nanny.

At the televisor, she clicked the nursery icon. "Nanny, please get Robbie ready to go out."

The lock clicked as she closed the office door behind her. Nanny was helping Robbie pull the fur coverings over his shoes. Her eyes were red.

Ilane said, "I'm taking him to the sweet shop."

Robbie grinned at her. "Really, Mama?"

"Yes, just the two of us. Isn't that a nice plan? Give Nanny a hug and say good-bye."

He flung his arms around Nanny's thick waist. "Bye, Nanny. I'll bring you some candy."

As they went out, Robbie reached for Ilane's hand and said, "Nanny was crying. Why was she crying?"

"I don't know. She didn't tell me." She didn't know, although she suspected Nanny had heard about Robbie. How did the servants always know everything? "It was kind of you to think of getting her a treat."

In a few moments they passed to Center Dome and left the slidewalk to stroll through the marketplace where the shop windows were bright in the afternoon half-light.

Ilane pressed a coin into the boy's hand. "You may spend that on yourself." Then another coin. "And that's for Nanny's treat. I'm going to make a call on the public telecomm just outside the shop."

She waited long enough to see him walking down an aisle, head swinging back and forth as he tried to look at everything at once, fingers curled tightly around the coins.

Then she closed the booth door and punched in her parents' estate number. They would take care of everything. The screen wavered, then focused on her mother, kneeling on a cushion and arranging moonflowers in a vase.

"How is my mother?"

"Very well, thank you. And how is my daughter?"

"Well indeed. Is my father in good health?"

"Yes, his arthritis is better. He's seeing the foreman. He'll be sorry to miss talking to you."

Ilane wasn't sure what to say next. "Have you heard about the genes at the lab?"

"Yes, it was on the bulletin. It's very sad, all those children contaminated." A flower dropped from her hand, and her eyes widened. "Is Robbie—?"

"He received the wrong batch. Tomorrow my husband will call the enforcers, and they'll take Robbie away."

"Oh. What a terrible turn of fate. Poor thing, poor boy."

Ilane rushed on. "May we come and hide on the estate? The cabin in the mountains…"

Her mother's forehead creased, and her eyes looked down as she interrupted, "You must do as your husband tells you. He knows what is best."

"No, Mother. Robbie's just a boy. I can't let them take him away. Please help us, please, Mother, please. I can rent a ground car. No one would know."

Her mother's hands fluttered. "Your father would be so angry. We must obey the law. And so must you. There is…"

"Sign off." The screen went blank. Never before had Ilane been so rude as to sign off without leave-taking. For a moment she stood shaking, but she couldn't help Robbie if she gave way to rage. She forced herself to close her eyes and breathe deeply. *I am a mountain lake, smooth and serene.*

The dome had darkened, and the globe lamps were brightening. The store was crowded with after-work shoppers, and when she didn't see Robbie right away, she began to panic, shoving her way through people blocking the aisles. When she finally spotted him, he was holding a pink-

and-white striped bag and inspecting a display of marshmallow animals. "I think Nanny would like a rabbit."

She took a minute to calm herself, then said, "That sounds lovely."

While he was paying for the rabbit, she was thinking hard. Out on the concourse, he plunged his hand into the bag and stuffed a caramel into his mouth. "Mmm. Are we going home now?"

"Don't talk with candy in your mouth. We have an errand to run."

They passed the bookshop where Ilane had spent many hours browsing the shelves trying to find books she hadn't read before. Not even her husband knew how many books she had devoured.

A clerk was standing on a step stool reaching down a book for a customer. For the first time, Ilane thought she might like to be a member of the lower classes. There would be no worry about genetic lines. She could work in a bookshop and wouldn't have to wear ankle chains that chafed her skin and forced her to take tiny, lady-like steps.

Holding Robbie's hand, she walked through the airlock into a lobby with a gray marble floor and split bamboo walls. People were streaming out among mingled odors of perfume and sweat, furs and woolens.

Ilane spoke to the man at the greeter desk. "I am Lady Ilane, wife of Shiyo. I'd like to see the Commissioner of Genetic Purity, please."

"Do you have an appointment?"

"No, but my husband is a friend of his."

If she could only make the commissioner understand, he would fix things for Robbie, and they could go home. She would apologize over and over again to her husband, and after a time he would forgive her.

The greeter clicked on an icon and relayed the information, then turned to Ilane. "He says you're to go to his office. Go past the moving stairs and then turn right."

The commissioner was standing in the doorway to his office, a short, slender man. "Welcome, my lady. It is good to see you again."

Ilane inclined her head. "I hope I'm not delaying you."

"Not at all. I will be working late tonight, because of the problem at the lab."

Ilane pulled Robbie in front of her and put her hands on his shoulders. "This is my husband's son."

Robbie politely offered his hand, but the commissioner glanced at him sharply without shaking it. "I think I see."

Ilane motioned toward a bench beneath a white-barked tree in a container and told Robbie, "Sit there and don't move. You may eat more candy. I must speak to the commissioner in private."

The commissioner went into his office and stood at the sideboard. "May I offer you some tea?"

Ilane chose a chair facing the man's desk and pulled off her gloves, dropping them in her lap. "No, thank you."

He moved behind the desk, settled in his chair, and, clasping his hands on the desktop, said, "What do you wish to say to me?"

Ilane tried to speak softly and reasonably, but she heard the edge of desperation in her voice. "Robbie got a bad batch of fa Liri genes, but it's not his fault. He's just a boy. He needs to be at home."

The commissioner replied, "Impossible. All of those children must be segregated."

Her hands tightened around each other. "But an exception could be made. You and my husband are friends."

"I'm sure your husband does not know you are here. He is a man of honor and would never ask for special treatment."

Ilane reached into her sash and began to toss notes onto the desk. "I brought money. I brought jewels."

The commissioner drew back. His voice became icy. "This is unworthy of you. I shall have to inform your husband. Go. Leave my office."

Her face hot, tears prickling in her eyes, Ilane stood and wadded the money back into her sash. The commissioner opened the door for her without a word.

Robbie was still sitting on the bench, kicking his legs. "Was that man mean to you?"

Ilane sank down next to him. "I just don't know what to do. But don't worry." She wiped her eyes on a handkerchief and blew her nose. "Let's just sit here for a moment while I think. Look, you can see the trader ship from here, all lit up, and the crew loading it." She fell silent, absently rubbing her ankle.

It was up to her to save Robbie. There was no one else to turn to, nowhere to go.

Robbie said knowledgeably, "They check the seams and the engines. And it's not the actual ship, it's a shuttle. The big ship is in orbit with all the families on it."

"How smart you are," Ilane said, "to know so much."

"I saw it on the vidnews with Papa. They're getting ready to leave." He sighed. "I wish I could go."

Abruptly Ilane stood up. "Come."

They went back through Center Dome. The crowds in the concourse were thinning as people returned home for their evening meal. It was getting to be so late; had her husband awakened yet? Maybe he had called the enforcers to pick her up and Robbie. Or maybe the commissioner had called. She chose the passage around the perimeter of the dome, where there were fewer people, and the lamps were farther apart. It was also colder, and her breath puffed white in front of her mouth. She wanted to hurry, but the bracelet cuffs cut into her ankles, and the chain made her stumble.

Outside Dome 3, the trader shuttle lay in its cradle, looking like a fish with stubby fins, lights glaring off its hull. Swarming around it, some on the ground, others in hoists at its flanks, were people in protective orange suits, the helmets down. A hatch gaped open to receive crates that a crane loaded one by one.

A fabric tunnel connected the dome's airlock to the shuttle. Stationed at its entrance was a man who held a device in his hand, jabbing it with a stylus. A young man in tunic and breeches staggered by in a cloud of beer fumes. With a feeling that she'd been turned inside out, Ilane saw that what she had taken to be a man was a woman, her hair cut short, dressed in breeches, who had evidently been drinking in the lower levels.

The man with the stylus turned to Ilane. "Yes?"

"I would like to arrange transportation—that is, I—" she hesitated, unsure what to say.

The man frowned and spoke slowly. "A trade you wish? We go soon. No more trades."

Two people came down the hall, a boy around Robbie's age and a man whose tunic bore some kind of insignia. The boy stopped in front of Robbie and reached out a hand. Ilane started forward, but the boy only fingered Robbie's fur jacket. Then he went to the dome wall and gestured to Robbie. They stood together, the boy pointing outside and chattering in a foreign language.

Ilane drew herself up and spoke to the guard in her most imperious manner. "I must see the captain."

He frowned. "Captain busy. Very, very busy."

"Then someone else. Someone important."

The other man pointed to his insignia and said, "I am the chief trader." He had an accent, drawing out the vowels, but Ilane had no difficulty understanding him.

"Robbie!"

"I don't want to leave, Mama."

"I'm going to talk to this man. Stay right there."

The trader opened a door set into the wall. A room held chairs with thin cushions and a plain wooden table. "This room is for trading—for the negotiations. Sit down, please."

She sat in the closest chair and drew a deep breath. *I am a mountain lake.*

The man sat on the other side of the table and leaned back. "Your wish, what is it?"

Ilane clasped her hands in her lap. Should she beg him for mercy? Offer him the jewels? At last, she simply said, "I have money. I want to buy passage on your ship for myself and my son."

He held up a hand, palm forward. "Always there is someone who is trying to run away. It makes problems, for them, for us. We have a rule— no passengers."

"But you see, we must go. We'll get off at the next planet."

"Next stop is Rigel 10. Not for enjoying, no, not at all."

"Then somewhere else."

"You would stay with the ship, and after a while you would cry and cry to go home. Our schedule is to return to this planet in a few years. To us, a few years, because we travel fast, close to the speed of light.

Groundside, many, many years, because time goes forward at a different rate. That is why our families with us come. For you, everyone you know, parents, friends—husband?—all dead and ashes."

"But you use wormholes that take you from one part of the galaxy to another in the blink of an eye."

"Ah, but we have to get to and from the wormholes." He made a shooing motion with his hands. "Go home now and work out whatever needs to be worked out."

She began to stack notes on the desk. He looked at the piles but made no move to touch them. Opening her bag, she took out a necklace that swirled onto the cheap wood, where it gleamed with gold, and then the other pieces of jewelry one by one until the bag was empty.

He eyed them, and she had the sense that he was adding up the values. "This is not a pleasure ship, madam. You have a maid? On the ship, no one to pick up your handkerchief when you drop it. No shops to pass time. Everyone has a job."

"I will do a job."

"You have what skills? What can you do for us?" He quirked an eyebrow and smiled a little, as if confident she had no reply.

She was silent. After all, what could she do? Write exquisite poems, arrange flowers, give orders to the cook. Strange that it had never before occurred to her that she couldn't do anything useful. Her eyes darted around the bare little room trying to find inspiration.

Hesitantly she said, "When you trade here, it is polite to offer tea and cakes. The room should be decorated with pictures and a vase of flowers. That shows respect." Her mind worked frantically to come up with another example, and she remembered a book from the shop. "On Rigel 10, gifts must be exchanged before any trading can begin. I can learn the customs of a port before we land, to prepare you for the bargaining."

A knock came on the door. The guard stuck his head in and spoke a few words, then left.

The trader said, "My nephew reminds me that we are leaving soon." He paused, giving her a look as if assessing her value. "You are sure you wish to come?"

Her mouth dry, Ilane nodded, then croaked out, "Yes."

The man chuckled. Picking up the gold necklace and a ring with a cluster of rubies, he pushed the rest back toward her. "You bargain well. These will pay for the first part of the journey, for you and your son to know the ship. After that you work, and we pay you."

She returned the rest of the jewels to her bag and once again tucked the money into her sash, her fingers shaking; she couldn't tell if it was with fear or excitement. She went out and called to Robbie.

"Mama, I saw them loading the shuttle, and one of the crates almost fell, but the man stopped it."

She knelt in front of him and adjusted his coat. "We're going on the shuttle and leaving on the ship."

"We're going on the shuttle? Really, Mama?"

"Yes, dear. And it might be a long time before we return."

His forehead crinkled. "I won't see Nanny to give her the rabbit?"

"No, dear, because the shuttle is leaving soon."

"Can I give it to Mariño?"

"Is that your new friend? Yes, that would be nice."

Robbie and Mariño ran down the tunnel. The trader waited for Ilane to go ahead of him. She stooped and unfastened first one ankle cuff, then the other. Straightening, she drew back her arm and heaved them against the dome wall, where they struck with a thud and a jangle. Then she turned and strode through the open doorway.

one doll missing—
the other smiles,
crumb of stuffing on her mouth

Whispers

When Mom was pregnant, she got thinner and bonier as her belly got bigger and bigger. She ate pies, French fries, fried chicken. One day she asked for a bunch of Slim Jims, and Dad was tired, so I trudged to the 7-11, wishing I was three years older and had my driver's license. By the time I got back, Mom was so hungry she tore the wrappers open with her teeth, one after the other.

The baby was so big the doctor had to do a C-section. Dad put on a mask and gown and went into the operating room. I called the neighbor lady to ask her to feed the dog and then sat in a waiting room that smelled like old coffee. Finally an aide came to get me. "This way," she said, and strode down the hall, me scurrying behind.

The baby barely fit into the crib, puffs and folds and puddles of fat, and he was whimpering thin, choked-up cries. "Is everything okay?" I asked. "What did you name him?" Mom and Dad looked at each other and sent me out into the hall so they could whisper.

When they let me back in, I picked up the baby, but his flesh was cold through the swaddling blanket. "Poor cold baby," I crooned, trying to warm him in my arms. He kept crying.

Even after he came home from the hospital, his flesh was always waxy-white and cold, and blankets couldn't warm it. Mom gave him bottles, and he spit out the formula.

A couple of months after the baby came home I noticed two thin teeth poking out from between his lips, like fangs.

And he cried and cried, this choked-up whimpering. One night Dad couldn't stand it any longer and tried to hold his jaws together. He sank a fang into Dad's wrist and latched on, and Dad had to pull him off. The hand swelled up and turned bright red. Dad had to go to the hospital and get a tetanus shot and an IV full of antibiotics. That cost a lot of money. And ever since, his hand aches, and he can't bend the fingers all the way closed, so he can't do the construction work.

About a month ago we moved into this dumpy trailer park in this dumpy trailer. The sides are spotted with rust, and the door sticks, and the greenish shag carpeting smells funny. There's not a lot of room, so Mom usually just plunks the baby on the floor.

Sometimes I try to play with the baby, patty caking on the bottoms of his feet or pumping his arms up and down, but I stop when he snaps at me.

A few days ago our dog disappeared. Maybe he ran off and got lost. Maybe a coyote got him. He was snappish and yappy, but the trailer was so quiet without him. The baby was quiet too.

Tonight Mom and Dad went into the bedroom and whispered. After a while Mom stuck her head out the door as if to check that I wasn't standing there with my ear to it.

I had been bent over the sticky fold-down table trying to do arithmetic homework, but I looked up. "What're you and Dad whispering about?"

From inside the bedroom Dad said, "None of your business."

Mom said, "Nothing, honey. Just—nothing."

The baby was crying. Dad yelled at me to shut it up.

"Nothing can shut that baby up."

Finally they said they were going out for a while. Dinner and a movie. Mom said, "You can use the ground beef in the fridge for supper."

"Okay. Have fun."

"We won't be back until late." She hugged me tight and didn't seem to want to let go. Dad stood at the door fiddling with the car keys and wouldn't meet my eyes.

I opened the refrigerator door and saw the red meat mounded under plastic wrap but ended up with a Tab and potato chips and munched while I watched some TV.

That was hours ago. It's after midnight now. Once in a while a car comes along on the road outside the trailer park, but the lights go on by, and it's not them. The baby is crying and staring at me with tears in his black eyes.

He's probably hungry. The last time I remember seeing Mom feeding him was last Wednesday, no, Tuesday when I came home from the library.

But she must be giving him something, or he would be starving. He wasn't crying yesterday. After the dog disappeared.

I'm staring back at the baby, thinking, and finally I sigh and go to the fridge. When I come back, the baby waves his hands in the air and opens his mouth. I stuff it with raw, red meat.

Crow flies
to the end of the world
and finds—
a mirror.

Visitation

It was not a happy village. Even the tramp who just arrived could see that. Men slouched down the main road, glancing at each other without making eye contact or smiling. Windows were closed despite the soft spring day, but curtains twitched as women peered out, suspicious of anyone who passed by.

Everyone was quarreling with someone else. Rob claimed that his neighbor Lorena's trumpet vine was strangling his roses. Lorena called him a fussy old bachelor. Marla and Katie, friends since they had shared a desk in the old schoolhouse 30 years ago, weren't speaking to each other. No one could quite make out what the problem was, although it seemed to involve a cake. If you asked one, she'd exercise her tongue as to how it was her recipe. If you asked the other, she'd let you know in no uncertain terms that she was the one who had baked it.

The blacksmith's wife was mad at him and every night served him meat burnt and black as the iron he shaped at the forge. Sisters tattled on brothers, and brothers slapped sisters and then had to draw water from the village well as punishment.

"But that's Sadie's chore."

"And no backchat from you." The mother wondered what she had done to deserve such quarrelsome children.

In most towns, when the tramp knocked on the back door of a prosperous-looking house, he'd get some leftover food and maybe do chores for a sleeping place in the shed. But here, the dogs were set upon him. He was running down the road, the dogs only one jump behind. He ran by the village green with its well, past the general store and the butcher's and the cobbler's, and the proprietors came to their doors to look and laugh at the sight. The biggest dog with the sharpest teeth was gaining.

The tramp was coming to the edge of town now, and the homes were becoming smaller and more tumbledown. One had a corner slumping over and a fence with pickets higgledy-piggledy, but a large garden with plants in neat rows. A woman stood at the open gate, motioning him in. He made a last effort and lunged through, and she closed the gate just in front of the biggest dog's nose. "Bad dog," she scolded in a gentle voice. "You go on home now." The dog went off, tail between its hind legs.

Then she turned to the tramp, who was bent over with his hands on his knees, sucking in air. "Come on inside," she invited. "I have soup warming on the fire." He followed her through a door that rattled on loose hinges, and she made him take off his jacket and sit on the softest chair. She limped to the fire and dished up some thin soup and put a large chunk of dark bread in it. As the tramp ate, she chose a needle and some thread and laid his jacket across her lap to mend the rips. "The people in town are not bad folks, but somehow they've forgotten what it's like to be cheerful, so they go around sour. Last summer when I broke my leg, neighbors brought me food and cleaned my house, but they grumbled the whole time. Fang, for one, wouldn't have bitten you, but he likes to scare strangers."

He asked if there was anything he could do to help. She said, "I can use help hoeing the garden. I've had to let the garden go a bit, but my supply of ingredients is sadly low." She showed him her stillroom with its clean, bright surfaces for working, the cabinets with packets and vials of remedies.

When the hoeing was done, she offered to give up her own bed to the tramp, but he said he'd be more comfortable on the back porch, looking up at the stars.

In the morning, he asked if there were any more chores he could do. She thought for a moment. "You could draw me some water. My leg is healing, but it still makes heavy work out of lugging that bucket."

He took the bucket to the village well and attached it to the hook. Cranking the windlass, he sent it down into the dark and brought it up filled. Bending over the bucket, he inhaled deeply and nodded in a satisfied way. Lorena was standing in back of him, shifting from foot to foot and muttering, "Don't take all day about it." He showed her the water, and she drew back, her nostrils pinched. Other people waiting in line edged closer. Someone muttered, "It smells delicious." A woman working in her garden saw them all gathered around the tramp and came to look, her children following behind. Then the butcher and the clerk at the general store wondered what the commotion was about and came outside. Soon there was a crowd around the bucket, but no one knew what to make of the sweet-smelling water.

The mayor ordered the herbwoman to be fetched. He shoved the bucket in front of her. She dipped a tin cup into the water, tasted it. In her gentle voice she said, "It's like drinking roses or a waterfall of wine, or a reflection of the sunrise…"

The mayor roared, "Can we drink it, woman?"

"Wait an hour and see how I feel."

People sat on benches around the well, glaring at each other, cuffing noisy children. Fang padded over to drink from the bucket, but Lorena threw a sandal at him.

After an hour, the herbwoman pronounced herself feeling fine. "Even better than fine. I feel happy. Content. And the ache in my leg went away."

Grumbling about the time wasted, and squabbling over their place in line, everyone filled their buckets and took them away. The tramp cupped his hands and scooped up some water so Fang could have a drink. The dog looked up at him apologetically as it lapped.

That evening the blacksmith's wife served him chicken and dumplings, with gravy like no one else could make. Her husband chased the last morsels around the dish with his spoon.

Rob knocked at Lorena's door and, when she opened it, held out three white rosebuds.

"The mayor told me they were cut from his prize-winning rosebush," Marla said when she ran into Katie in front of the general store.

Katie giggled. "I hear she invited him right on in." She resolved to buy dried-flower sachets from the herbwoman for Marla's birthday.

Sadie's brother mended her doll, and their mother sang as she washed dishes in the sweet-smelling water.

The next morning everyone awoke feeling more rested than they had in years. "Slept like a baby!" announced the blacksmith to his wife, pulling her closer in bed. His wife thought it was time they started to have children. Lots of children. She would go to the herbwoman for a fertility charm.

All that summer the town drank sweet water.

In the first weeks of autumn the water's aroma faded away. The entire village yawned with irritation and fatigue. They couldn't sit still at their tasks. They walked to the well, looked in and inhaled, but only got the scent of stone and cold. When they needed water, they took it reluctantly and snapped at the person in back of them to quit shoving. Even the dogs slunk around, dragging their tails, baring their teeth.

The mayor went to the herbwoman, who stood at her cabinet closing a white paper packet. Scents filled the air, pungent layered with spicy. He asked, "What are we to do, Elly?"

She shook her head, frowning. "I've gone all through my cabinet but can't find a match for it."

The mayor ran both hands through what was left of his hair. "I was just getting used to being happy. And not just me, everyone is going around so you can hardly say good morning without getting a strip of hide ripped off."

She hesitated. "There's a flower that grows in the mountains. It has a similar scent, although I've never heard of it having medicinal properties. But..."

The mayor looked at her, starting to smile. "If we sweetened the water with them..."

She nodded. "Then maybe people would think..."

The mayor said, "Don't just stand there as if you'd grown roots—come along!"

They walked through the village calling out. Everyone snatched up bags and baskets and slung babies onto their backs as they swarmed into the road. Children came running, holding the hands of toddlers who waddled on short fat legs. Dogs capered around, getting in everyone's way.

The tramp had been working in the herbwoman's garden. He stretched and took a stroll through the village, past the cobbler's shop—empty. The butcher's—empty. The general store—empty. No sound came from the smithy. He nodded to himself and went back to the herbwoman's house, where he finished the weeding.

As dusk was coming on, the villagers returned singing, cheeks brown with sun, arms full of flowers, baskets overflowing with flowers, flowers plumping out the sides of bags. Fang's neck bore two chains of flowers. They had enough to dry some and put them by for the winter.

At the well they gathered around and dropped flowers in. Then the mayor pulled up a bucket, giving it to the herbwoman for the first drink. She sipped and smiled, and the rest of the villagers stood politely in line to draw water, the windlass creaking steadily.

Rob carried Lorena's bucket. Marla and Katie shared a handle. The blacksmith, who had always scorned fetching water as women's work, drew two buckets to take home. He winked at the mayor as he murmured something about his wife having to take it easy for a few months. As Sadie offered her brother a drink, their mother whispered to the herbwoman, "We all know it's not the flowers. We need a little help, that's all."

The mayor offered his arm to the herbwoman. "That leg of yours must be tired. I'll help you home." When they reached her gate, he stammered, "I suppose you—would you—I'll come see you tomorrow—if you don't mind—" he turned and shot off in the direction of the village green. The herbwoman said softly, "Yes."

She strolled to the back, to sit in the garden, and saw the tramp cleaning the tools and putting them away. "You've left me nothing to do except get the water."

"I'll be doing that while you rest," he said.

She was tired from the long walk and sank down into the nearest chair. The tramp picked up a bucket and went into the road, calling a greeting to someone and getting a cheerful reply. His footsteps came back, and she heard the side of the bucket thunking against the lip of the tank, then the water rushing in.

She eased her feet out of her shoes, then took the flower out of her hair and twirled it, thinking about the mayor and slipping into a fond daydream.

It was so quiet she could hear the cooing of doves on the roof. How long had she been dreaming? Where was the tramp? He wasn't in the back. Running to the front gate, she looked left, then right, down the road out of town. Finally she spotted him. As he kept moving away, smaller and smaller, she told herself it must be the last of the afternoon sun shining on him that made him look as if he were filled with light.

Extravision Woman

Eyes up and down her arms,
eyes on her knees.
She lifts her hands:
    palms open
    eyes open.
An eye peers beneath
the hair on the back
of her head.
A tiny eye blinks
at the tip of her tongue.

Her heart is blind and tender.
Sometimes she closes
all her eyes
so she cannot see.

All the Deer Have Names

58

I remember riding the horse to the far pasture, just after sunrise, grass
 still damp. She stopped and pricked up her ears; I saw the deer over
 the fence, stopped, ears semaphoring toward us
I remember an entertainment park called Deer Forest, where we bought
 food pellets and the deer came up to us, tails flicking, and ate from
 our palms
I remember deer tracks in the snow, and following them into the woods,
 but I never saw the deer
I remember the first day of deer season, after Thanksgiving dinner, my
 cousin pulling orange quilted overalls over his shirt and pants and
 slinging his rifle case over his shoulder
I remember Grandma going down to the basement and leaning over the
 freezer and pulling out white paper packets of deer meat from deer
 Grandpa had shot
I remember a deer dead by the side of the road, pile of fur and legs, left
 behind after the car was towed away
I remember reading Bambi, and how all the deer had names

The Hunt

I don't remember being a baby in the incubator, and I don't really remember the foster home, although a couple of girls said there was a man with a loud laugh and a woman with gray hair, and a yard and a dog.

When we were five years old we were brought to the complex to be trained. Most days we sat in the same classroom. Day after day, month after month, year after year. At first we looked at pictures and were told stories. As we got older, it was reading and writing and numbers.

There was one basic message, repeated again and again. Always do as we were ordered. Only obey. Never say no.

When we were fourteen, we were taught housework—cooking, laundering, sewing, cleaning. We took on chores around the complex. I didn't mind doing chores.

Otherwise, our lives dragged in a circle—in the morning the guards took us from our sleeping rooms to the bathing room, then the dining room, followed by the classroom, the exercise room, the inner courtyard for sun, then the dining room, the bathing room, back to our sleeping rooms again.

We each had our own room with a narrow bed, a pisspot, in case we couldn't keep it in overnight, and shelves for our clothing and little treasures. A yellow bird feather I picked up in the courtyard. A sparkly pebble. A button from an outgrown dress. One year we were given dolls to help train us in baby care. I put mine on my bed. At night I'd tell her about the lessons or other things that happened during the day.

The guards mostly just did their job herding us around, but some were friendlier than others. Guard Lilla would sometimes talk to us, saying we were an investment, saying we were valuable, saying we should take advantage of our opportunities. It sounded like what they would tell us in class, but somehow it wasn't. Like there were words on top and something hidden below.

Once I overheard one of the other guards telling Guard Lilla she shouldn't talk to the merch so much. The boss wouldn't like it.

Guard Denny could get mean. Occasionally he'd slap us if we weren't quick enough to get in line or if we talked too loud. One morning as my chore group was lining up to go to the laundry, one of the girls—E-015—fell to the floor. Her eyes were rolled back. Guard Denny tried to pull her up by the arm, but she started thrashing around. He hit her. I ran over to try to pull him off. The girl was gasping, he was shouting at both of us, and girls were screaming. All the other guards came running.

We never saw Guard Denny again. We never saw that girl again either.

A couple evenings later as Guard Lilla closed me in my room, she said quietly, without looking at me, that the guards had orders not to damage the merchandise, and Guard Denny had been let go.

"And what about the girl?" I whispered.

"Genetic engineering's not as perfect as they lead their customers to believe."

"What will happen to her?"

Instead of answering, Guard Lilla buzzed the door locked.

When I took off my dress I found a tiny piece of paper in the pocket. On it were handwritten numbers in faded ink. They looked like communicator codes. In an hour they had faded completely. I thought about hiding the paper, but finally I realized that swallowing it would make sure it wasn't found.

When Guard Lilla came to get me for morning meal, I said, "I've memorized a lot of things, not just the alphabet. Numbers. Recipes."

"Have you now? That's good to know."

When we turned seventeen, we started to get work assignments. Girls would go and not come back. I was eager for my turn. I longed to get away, to see new things, new places. Finally the teacher announced to the class that I was getting a good position. "It's a married couple and a big estate. Wish her well, class."

There was a murmur of "fare-you-wells" as Guard Lilla and Nurse Kaie took me to a cubicle and laid me on a cot. Nurse Kaie gave me an injection. I felt tired and heavy. My eyes were closing as Guard Lilla pushed my doll into my arms.

Nils landed the hopper as smoothly as he could on the bumpy landing pad in back of the estate house, although there were a couple of woofs from the back in protest. He jumped out, a short, stocky man dressed in work woolens.

A man in a red uniform rode the glide ramp over from the pepperbush fields where anthros were bent over the rows of plants. "I'm the overseer. You must be Nils." He didn't offer to shake hands but looked Nils up and down. "You're older than I expected."

"Forty-seven years." Nils's philosophy was that it didn't do any good to get your back up.

"Did you bring the dogs like I told you?"

"Yes."

The overseer headed toward the house. "I'll show you the body, then you can get started tracking. It's in the study."

As they entered the back door, Nils caught a glimpse of a room to the right with furniture made of imported Earth woods and fabrics, but the overseer led him down the hall and thumbed a button on the wall. A heavy wooden door opened. "The body's in here," said the overseer, walking in and throwing himself into a leather chair, chewing on his mustache. "I don't need this when we're supposed to finish up the pepperbush contract this week and pick grapes in Nov Burgundy next week."

The room stank of blood and whiskey. A figure was sprawled in the middle of the floor, face down. Nils registered that the person was plump, with short graying hair. The back of the shirt was snowy-white, but blood had soaked into the reds and blues of the rug.

A cut-glass decanter lay sideways on the desk, smoky-gold liquid puddled around it. A jacket had been tossed carelessly onto the chair. One sleeve dangled over the chair's arm; the other sleeve brushed the floor.

The overseer went on, "This morning I came in with a question for Ser Grecin about the picking and found his body. Of course, I notified his wife and the Patrol and made inquiries. The wife was upstairs with a sick headache all morning, and the housekeeper was tending to her. No one else was in the house except for the anthro, and now she's gone. It's clear she killed him. And probably with his own knife, which is also gone."

The overseer gestured at the belt curled like a snake next to the body, its knife sheath empty. "Description, female anthropoid, seventeen years of age, skin fair, brown eyes, dark brown hair, 5 feet 4 inches. Identifying number and locator code 36263-85 E-010."

"E?"

"Experimental."

"What's experimental about her?"

"The line is being developed as a house anthro, doing kitchen chores, maid work, even child tending. Has to be smarter than the field hands."

"How much smarter?"

"About normal intelligence. The Labor Board approved it, all right and regular." His fingers dug into his mustache. "Anyway. The Patrol is demanding she be turned over to them for punishment, the lab wants her back to see what went wrong, and Rossel is looking to get its money's worth out of her, someway, somehow. And they're all chewing on my ass. In the meantime, we can't get a location from the anthro's chip because of the solar flares, so we'll have to track her with dogs. Everyone I talked to said to call Nils; he has the best hounds."

Nils said, "I breed and train dogs. Sometimes I track lost children, or dangerous animals."

"She's an anthro. If you refuse to help recover her, there are penalties. Don't think I'm afraid to use them." The overseer's mustache looked like a caterpillar that crawled and jerked as his mouth moved.

Nils knew the penalties. Loss of his license, his dogs—maybe even his farm. He rubbed his head and sighed.

His eyes followed a trail of reddish-brown drops that led to the patio. "She's injured," he said. "Self-defense, maybe?"

The overseer touched the electronic whip at his belt. "You can't have an anthro attacking a master. Not for any reason."

A woman swept into the room, skirt and petticoats rustling, jewels swinging at her ears. The make-up around her eyes was smeared. She thrust something at Nils. "You can use this to track her. Find her. Bring her back to face punishment." The doll was a shabby thing; the embroidery on the face almost worn away, the black yarn hair patchy.

"Seventeen years old and still playing with dolls, but she murdered my husband." Then the woman turned and hurried out.

Nils looked again at the jacket on the chair and the belt on the floor. Couldn't the woman see that her husband had attacked the anthro? Or maybe she didn't care?

The overseer stood at the patio door. The afternoon sun cast his shadow across the room, long arms and legs making it look like a spider. "Well?" he said.

Nils sighed again. "I'll get the dogs."

As he walked back to the landing pad, he noted the pepperbush fields and the anthros stepping and stooping, stepping and stooping, muscles outlined with sweat. Bored-looking guards stood at intervals, electronic whips dangling from their hands. On their sleeves they wore the red-and-white badge of the Rossel Company, the corporation that contracted to do planting and harvesting.

For the more delicate plants, like the pepperbush spice that was the planet's main export, anthro labor was cheaper than machinery, with less crop wastage. What wasn't talked about, what Nils hadn't thought about much, was that the anthros were engineered from human gene stock.

The dogs barked from their padded crates. The battered hatch door squeaked as he swung it up. Someday he'd find the time to fix it.

First he opened the gate for Patience, the bloodhound, who jumped down, long ears flapping, then nosed his hand. She would track anything to the world's end and back, then wag her tail and lick its face. Next he let out Giant, the shepherd-mastiff mix, who would guard and hold. Nils had bred and trained them both, and he felt a glow of pride as he watched them.

He kicked the ramp down for Molly, a genetically-engineered mare infused with camel genes for hardiness. She had cost him a lot of money but was worth every credit. He saddled her and tied bags to the pommel and cantle, lumpy with food and camping gear.

He told Molly and Giant to stay and took Patience to the house. The overseer stood on the patio, squinting up at the clouds billowing in from the north. He was speaking into his communicator. "No rain tonight, but rain tomorrow. We have to keep picking or the schedule will be blown to shit. Issue waterproofs to the guards."

Nils found where the spots of blood led away across the lawn. He held the doll out to Patience, who sneezed and then gave it a good sniff. He pointed to the blood trail. "There it is." She sniffed the trail with quivering nostrils, then looked up at him, tail wagging, forepaws shifting eagerly. He lifted his arm. "Find it." Patience put her nose to the ground and trotted away.

Nils went to Molly and Giant. Putting a foot in the mare's stirrup, he swung into the saddle. The overseer called, "Report tonight. I expect to hear progress."

Beams of sun broke through the masses of grayish-white clouds as Nils nudged the mare into a lope to catch up to Patience. Giant ran beside the mare.

When they got into the hills, they slowed to a walk, following Patience on a game trail around rocks and catclaw bushes. Molly was steady and smooth, and Nils clicked up a map on his communicator. The hills piled higher and higher, then leveled out into a plateau. Midway across the plateau was Port City. The girl was probably headed there. She would be able to find work, buy identity papers, then lose herself. He glanced up at the silvery spark that hung in the sky, the satellite in geosynchronous orbit over the city.

The light dimmed and faded, and it was time to think about making camp for the night. He was happy to spot an umbrella tree, bare trunk topped with long leathery leaves that were starting to lower down for the night. It would provide a shelter as good as a tarp.

When they stopped, his first concern was taking care of the animals. He gave the dogs water and strips of dried meat and brushed them, checking them for insects and untangling the catclaw burrs. Then Molly got a good brushing before he let her loose for the night. She wouldn't go far. She nosed the vegetation, even though she didn't need to eat for a couple days. He heard her pawing.

When he investigated, Nils saw she had found some water plants. He peeled the gray-green nodules and chewed on the pulp. It tasted like wet cardboard, but the nodules would be a welcome supplement to his water supply.

His hired hands must have finished the evening chores by now. He tried calling Dusty but got only static. Dusty was a good manager. What would happen to Dusty and the others if Nils didn't re-capture the anthro? It wasn't so easy to find good jobs.

He queued up a message for Dusty and a brief report for the overseer. They would go through whenever there was a respite from the solar flares.

As he bit into a bland nutrition stick, Nils anchored a ground cover under the tree and set out his sleeping roll. He thought about eating another nutrition stick, but he was trying to keep his weight under control.

He took the doll out of his pack. Although worn, it was clean. A rip in its side had been mended with tiny, precise stitches. The way he figured it, this doll was well-loved. The only thing the anthro had to care about.

Leaves rustled under Molly's hooves. Patience woofed in her sleep. Everyday peaceful sounds. Nils stretched out in the sleeping roll and put his hands beneath his head, staring up at the sheltering leaves.

Had the anthro found shelter? Seventeen years old. He had never made the time to find a sweetheart, get married, have children. If he had, he might have a daughter the girl's age. Just a child, really. Normal intelligence, in an anthro. As smart as he was. And the Labor Board had approved it.

First-light woke him, and he was ready to go in minutes. He held up the doll for Patience to sniff, and she set right out.

The girl was keeping to the trail. The dogs trotted slowly, their long-distance trot, and the mare kept up with them, winding her way among rocks that became larger and larger, and treading on tiny plants that sent up a minty fragrance. Occasionally Nils saw the girl's slender footprints on the softer earth beside the trail.

Once Patience made a detour off the trail. When he got off the mare to inspect the ground, he noted trampled grass and loose dirt, where evidently the anthro had eliminated and covered it up. Just a small amount, hardly anything. He wondered if she had found food, water.

A squeal from his pocket told Nils the comm channel was open. Last night's messages had gone out.

His fingers clicked impatiently over the keys until Dusty answered. "What's going on at the farm?" Nils asked. "How are Bonnie's pups?" After receiving a report, he gave instructions on the day's work and on repairing the paddock fence.

Dusty said, "It'll be a bit of money to repair. We could put up some wire instead."

"No, it's better to do it right," Nils replied. "Good to hear about Bonnie's pups. I'll call in when I can. Let me know if anything comes up." He clicked off.

The comm started to blink as it picked up the girl's locator signal; she couldn't be far away. Locators were good at indicating a general area, although they did not pinpoint very well. He hesitated, then loosened the gun in the holster under his arm.

He patted the air in a downward motion. "Giant, Molly, wait. Wait. Patience, find it."

She woofed and walked over to a boulder, nostrils flaring and contracting. She shuffled left, then right, whining. Finally she pawed at the boulder. Nils clambered up, boots slipping on the stone. Still he couldn't spot the girl. Patience's paws scrabbled as she tried to find a way between the boulders. The next boulder had a pile of brown leaves at its base. Maybe the girl had made her bed there. He almost jumped down, and then the leaves fluttered up and away. Rock bats. His stomach clenched.

"Patience! Back! Back!"

Rock bats had needle teeth that could pierce an animal's skin, and then the fangs pumped in a substance that turned the animal's flesh to mush so the bats could suck it out. They mostly fed on dead animals, but there were reports of them attacking living creatures.

Dreading what he might find, he leaned over to look more closely. He could make out the imprint where a body had lain, and dark, dried splotches on the grass. That was what had attracted the rock bats, the blood. But since there was no body, they had left.

He scrambled down, scanning the area nervously in case the bats returned. A glint caught his eye. Between two pebbles rested a metal wafer with four prongs, bits of flesh clinging to them. He pictured the girl with the stolen knife in her hand, cutting into her arm, slicing down to the locator chip and prying it out.

Seventeen years old, but gutsy. And smart, to know she had to get rid of the chip.

He panned the comm over the scene and sent it to the overseer, with a brief "The anthro got rid of the locator chip."

A drop of rain spattered his cheek. The rain predicted by the overseer was here. As if triggered by his thought, the comm beeped, and the overseer's face flickered on. "I got your message about the chip. Damn, that'll leave a scar. Not that it matters now. Just get her back." His caterpillar mustache twitched.

"Right." Nils punched off the comm. He made his way back to where the animals were waiting.

Nils guessed that the girl would go through the boulders for a while, then get back on the trail to Port City. He set Molly down the trail, calling for the dogs to come. In a few hundred meters Patience picked up the girl's scent again, woofing happily.

The trail sloped down to a stream. The mare lowered her haunches and half-slid down. The dogs waded into the stream and stood lapping water ruffled by wind and rain.

Maybe the girl had waded up or down the stream to hide her trail. He could go back to the overseer and say the anthro had lost them at the water. The dogs reached the bank on the other side, then stood shaking themselves, water spraying from their coats.

Patience cast around and found the scent again, looking back at Nils with one paw curled up, whining eagerly.

"Patience! Giant!" The dogs looked at him, tips of their tails wagging. He opened his mouth to call them back, then closed it. If the overseer learned he had let the girl go, he could lose everything. May as well let the rock bats suck him dry.

He put his heels to the mare, sending her splashing across the stream.

Fresh in the soft streambank he found the prints of two goats, overlaid by the girl's footprints. They were small and slender. They looked so vulnerable. He envisioned the overseer sneering at her, his mustache crawling over his upper lip. The Patrol leading her away, not gently.

His legs hurt, his back hurt, and it was raining. He was getting to be too old for tracking.

Nils swung down off the horse and chose a pack. He dumped in most of the nutrition sticks and all of the water nodules. Medical patches for her arm. Holding up a pair of coveralls, he fingered a hole where one of Bonnie's pups had chewed, but they were better than nothing, so he put them in the bag too. All the coins he had. He fastened the bag's seal and paused, then tied the doll on top. After strapping the pack on Patience, he said, "Bring it to the girl. To the girl." He gestured at the trail, and Patience set off. Giant would have followed, but Nils called the dog over and stood smoothing his ears. "We'll wait for Patience to come back."

The rain eased to hardly more than mist when Patience belled a long call, then began to bark anxiously. Giant leaped up and whined. Nils leaped onto the mare. "Let's go see what's what."

They found Patience at the edge of a grassy meadow, picking up her forepaws and putting them down, nervous. The bag was gone, and Nils felt his heart lift. Had the girl taken it?

In the meadow a pile of dead leaves fluttered, but there was no wind. With a start, Nils realized it was a cluster of rock bats, feeding. The massing of bats showed it to be about the size of a girl. There was even the outline of a limb stretched out stiff and straight. He choked out, "No." Leaning over Molly's neck, he took deep breaths. The bats' wings rustled. A goat bleated from the rocks.

After a few minutes Nils straightened in the saddle. The pack was gone. There had been two goats at the stream, but only one had bleated. Bats didn't usually attack living animals. He chose to hope. "Farewell, little girl, wherever you fare."

Nils recorded the scene on his comm along with a remark that the anthro had met her end. He tried to send it. Nothing but static. He put it in the queue, then turned the mare and called the dogs.

He rode most of the night, stopping only a few times to rest and feed the animals. When he arrived at the estate, the Patrol questioned him and took the recording. They planned to go and examine the body, until a hijacking on the southern continent drew them away.

In the study, the overseer stood in the middle of the rug, one foot on the faint stain that remained. He sneered. "I don't know as I could recommend you for more anthro-tracking jobs."

Nils said nothing but stared at the man's mouth, fighting an urge to drive his fist into that crawling caterpillar mustache.

When Nils finally got out of the study, he loaded the dogs and the mare into the hopper and headed home.

Several months later, Nils sat with his feet up on his scarred desk, reading the anti-genetic engineering pamphlet the fellow at the feed depot had given to him. From time to time he wiped his forehead with a handkerchief. It was the dry season, baking hot.

Part of his mind registered familiar noises. One of the men whistling, a shout from the training paddock: "Up, boy. Up." Dogs barking an alert. He put down the pamphlet.

A knock came on the door frame. A drifter hesitated in the doorway, a boy in faded coveralls. A much-mended pack bowed his shoulders. He pulled off his cap and clutched it in front of him with both hands. A long, dark-brown braid fell over one shoulder, and Nils realized it was a girl. Her face and hands were dark with sun, her throat fair, the neck looking too thin to hold up her head.

"I've come looking for a job. I don't mind heavy work." Her voice was soft, gentle.

He tapped his fingers on the desk. There were always chores drifters could help with, but if they didn't seem like they'd fit in, he gave them money and sent them on their way.

"Where are you from?"

"Port City, originally. After that, here and there."

This girl was so young. He'd bet she was a runaway. "It's a hard life, drifting, especially for a girl. My advice for you is to go back home to your family."

"I don't have a family," she said. "And I like being…" her voice dropped so low he almost didn't catch the word "free."

Maybe she just needed a job. "Why do you want to work here?"

"I like dogs. A dog helped me once when I needed it." A pause. "I'm stronger than I look."

Nils nodded at the pack. "Got your papers in there?"

She slid the straps off her arms and rummaged in the pack, handing him documents with seals and signatures. Nils took them, then his hand froze. His eyes had snagged on her half-open pack, the water bottle, half a bag of food bars, and a doll, the girl's hand smoothing its black yarn hair.

Cradle Spell

place two rectangles of white linen
on top of each other

sew them together along three edges
pulling each stitch tight
so it can't be broken

tuck her inside
and then you can sew the bottom
closing it like a cocoon

coo and whisper over
the mysterious bulges and hollows
(is this a knee is that the mouth)

press the bundle to your milky breast

this is how to keep her
keep her small
keep her always

Honeybread

72

Every month the family went to the City of the Dead, walking what seemed to the two girls to be miles and miles from their home in the village. They knew they were getting close when they could see the top of the gate, its iron shafts arrowing up. Then they saw the tiny cottage where the gatekeeper lived and heard the honeywoman chirping, "Honeybread? Honeybread?" The girls always begged their parents to buy some, but the parents almost always said no. And then they passed the gatekeeper standing at the open gate, his hood pulled down so low the girls had never seen his face.

The familiar gravel paths to the family restinghouse took them past some of their favorite monuments—the lady looking at the sky, the tall stone with a gilded sun set into the face, and the child with her arms full of carved, stone roses.

The Mercy Stone was farther in, and whenever the girls went exploring they avoided it. A dark twilight always filled the grove, and the slab of marble looked like a hard, cold bed. Ebio, the older sister, said to her mother, "It's sort of scary." Her mother replied that some people found peace there.

When they arrived at the family restinghouse, Ebio helped her mother set out the food, putting some into the offering bowl and pouring wine on the ground for the gods. She was eight years old, and she was proud of the responsibility. Sagira was only four and had to rest after the long walk.

After they had eaten, their father went to check the restinghouse and stones for weather damage and to talk with neighbors. Their mother chanted the Remembrances to ease the ancestors' spirits down death's river.

Ebio knew one day she would be the one to Remember the ancestors. She understood the form and had memorized some of the words. "Halima the kind-hearted would give away anything she had. Beggars knew to go to her door for food."

Ebio knew one day she would be grown and have a husband as handsome as Father. She would cook the food lovingly and bring her flock of children to the City. As many children as she could manage, the older ones helping the younger ones.

One of the sacred sundogs slipped through the grove of trees farther up the hill. Ebio jumped up. "Look, Sagira! A sundog! Let's go after it." Whenever the girls saw a sundog, they ran after it, hoping to pet it, but the dogs always eluded them.

Sagira said, "Tired." Her face was pale and moist.

"You probably need more to eat," Ebio said. She handed Sagira her own handful of dates. Sagira shook her head and stuck her thumb in her mouth.

Partway home, Sagira held her arms up to her father to be carried. He said, "It's a long way to carry you. Can you walk a little farther?" She shook her head no and held up her arms again.

When a few days went by, and Sagira didn't get better, they asked the village healer to visit. The healer didn't know what to do. They asked a healer from the city on the river, who shook his head and said it was a rare disease.

The parents consulted other healers, a witchwoman—even the Holy Seer. They paid for rubbings with herbal ointments. They bought costly medicines, pills of poison to kill the sickness, and Sagira cried and retched and said the room wouldn't stop moving. They paid for bleedings. Ebio watched Sagira scream and try to pull away and hit the bleeder when he unsheathed the small, glittering knife—but she was held firm until bright blood leaped into his metal basin. Friends and neighbors chanted prayers for her, burned incense, and gave her gifts.

Ebio sang to Sagira and told her stories, but Sagira became sicker and weaker, sometimes spending all day in bed, tensing every few minutes as pain rippled through her body. Her skin broke out in red, itchy patches. Her curls came out in clumps.

One day Ebio heard the grown-ups talking about a new treatment that might extend Sagira's life a few more months although it would leave her paralyzed. She went into the bedroom where Sagira lay, holding a new doll and murmuring lullabies in a voice made hoarse by the healer's latest potion.

Ebio said, "They want to try cutting along your backbone and packing it with healing herbs."

Sagira started to whimper. "No cut. No."

"Shhh. If you want me to, I'll take you to the City of the Dead."

Sagira stopped crying long enough to think about it. "Get honeybread?"

Ebio remembered the coins she had been given for the River Mother's celebration day. "As much as you can eat." She warned, "You can't come back. It'll be like—" she tried to think how grown-ups described death. "—like falling asleep, and never waking up."

"I go."

"Are you sure?"

"Yes."

Ebio waited until everyone else had gone to sleep, then gathered up their wraparounds, fleecy and warm against night chills, tied her bag of coins at her waist, and stole a knife from the kitchen for protection. The girls slipped out the back, Ebio leading, holding her sister's hand and steadying her when she stumbled. They went very slowly and stopped often to allow Sagira to rest. Ebio let her sit for a while, then managed to coax her along, but the time between rests became shorter and shorter.

It was long after midnight when they came to Trader's Crossing. Two men came staggering down the roadway, holding each other up and singing untunefully. Ebio pulled Sagira behind some tall grasses until the men had passed. When they had gone and she couldn't hear them anymore, she tugged at Sagira's hand.

Sagira didn't want to get up. "Tired." Her breath rasped in her throat, and her forehead was cold with sweat. Ebio knew she had guessed wrong about Sagira's strength. The girl couldn't possibly walk all the way to the City. Ebio's lips trembled. Stupid. She had been stupid. Now what to do?

An ox-cart creaked its way up the road and halted in front of them. Ebio couldn't make out the man's face, but he had a smooth tenor voice. "Do you want a ride?"

"Where are you going?"

"I have some business at the City of the Dead."

"That's where we're going," said Ebio. She added, "I have a knife."

The man's teeth flashed, he put his head back, and shouted with laughter so that Ebio felt herself smiling with him.

He said, "There are empty sacks in the back. You two climb on top of them to soften the ride." Ebio boosted Sagira over the sideboards, then scrabbled in herself, keeping an eye on the man. He sat on the driver's seat holding the reins, not even looking back at them. Sagira lay down quietly on the sacks, seemingly content. The oxen leaned into the harness, and the creak of wheels soothed Ebio's fears.

Dawn light began to seep into the sky, turning the clouds pink and amber. Now Ebio saw that the two oxen were pure white, and the man was dressed in good, dark linen clothing. She spotted the tops of the City's arrowed shafts.

The driver pulled up the oxen by the gatekeeper's cottage. Ebio got out, moving stiffly, and helped Sagira down, brushing some hay off her skirt.

Turning to thank the man, Ebio saw that he was the Gatekeeper, his hood pulled low over his face. She said, "I'm sorry. I didn't know." She thought he was smiling.

"No need to be sorry." He pulled out a key like a sliver of glass, and the gate opened with no more noise than a metallic whisper. He gestured to the girls with a grand sweep of his arm, as if they were royalty he was inviting to enter.

The honeywoman held out her basket and chirped, "Honeybread? Honeybread?"

Ebio gave the honeywoman all of her coins, and the woman filled their hands with golden, sticky rolls. The children walked into the City of the Dead stuffing their mouths with sweetness.

They came to the Mercy Stone, flushed pink with sunrise. Birds made glad morning sounds. The girls put the bread they hadn't been able to finish in an offering bowl.

A sundog trotted up and nibbled on a roll. They watched in silence, barely breathing. It walked over to them and let them stroke its golden, silky fur. It put its cold black nose in their hands, licking off the honey.

When the hands were licked clean it curled up at the foot of the Mercy Stone.

Sagira said, "You come."

Ebio realized that since the beginning of the journey—in fact, since she had offered to bring Sagira here—she had known this moment would come. And knew her decision. But she had to take a moment to run through her dreams one more time. Her handsome husband, all those unborn children. Then she let them float away. "Yes." Ebio put her wraparound on top of the stone.

Sagira lay down on the Mercy Stone and let out a sigh so deep it seemed to come from her toes. She rolled onto her side facing Ebio and put her thumb in her mouth.

Ebio settled next to her, pulling Sagira's wraparound over them both. She put an arm over Sagira's shoulder. She whispered, "Sagira the Sick had a sister named Ebio, who loved her more than words can tell…"

In a few minutes, they fell asleep. And did not wake.

God as a Swarm of Bees

A dark, shrieking cloud
burning your skin with stings.

Sticky gold packed into waxy combs.
You pull off pieces and eat.

Anger and sweetness—
the taste of honey
those stings of fire.

Shagreeta

Keldara was twelve years old when she dedicated herself to Shagreeta, the Leopard Goddess.

One day she and her twin brother had been playing a game of tap-stones in the courtyard, a game Keldak almost always won. This time, he was letting her win. It made her feel soft because he loved her enough to lose. But it also made her cross, because she wanted to win truly. She tossed the stones in the air. "No one wins." He laughed, and then he started to cough and couldn't stop. She thumped his back. She got him a cup of water. When the coughing didn't stop, she ran to get her mother.

Days later he was still coughing, black hair damp with sweat, brown eyes reddened. Each cough rasped Keldara's heart as she placed cool cloths across his forehead or tried to spoon broth into his mouth. Mother's eyes despaired as she brewed an herbal tea for him. Father stayed home, pacing up and down the sleeping room instead of riding out to check on the herds.

He turned to Keldara. "You've been here all night and all morning. Go. Rest."

"I'm not tired."

"Go."

Keldara hesitated, then slipped out the door. She hurried to the outside walkway and passed under the vine-covered arch to the family chapel. Nailed to the door frame was a silver hand, palm outwards, indicating that inside the door, human and divine could meet. Touching her hand to the silver one, palm to palm, Keldara murmured, "I ask for your blessings, now and always." She pushed the door open.

The windows were shuttered, and the chapel's dimness soothed her eyes. On holy days, of course, Mother would light rows and rows of candles, but this morning only the white globe of the moon candle glowed. The flame never went out. Her father's grandfather had brought it back from his pilgrimage to the monastery high in the northern mountains.

On the far wall hung the family's greatest treasure, a tapestry that illustrated the adventures of the hundred gods and goddesses, both the minor and major deities. Sendo Iron Eagle, god of justice, opening his beak in a scream. His sister, Aruna Snow Dove, goddess of mercy. Khelet Otter on the bank of a river, laughing into good humor the thieves who had waylaid him. Keldara's eyes went to Shagreeta Leopard, who had always been her favorite deity. The tapestry showed her leaning over a child dying of fever, the dark rosettes on her gray fur seeming to stir as she breathed life into the girl.

A stone altar stood in front of the tapestry. This morning it was piled with field lilies, their orange cups sweetening the air, offerings from the family, the house servant, and the herders. But Keldak still coughed.

Keldara knelt on the wooden floor before the altar. "Goddess," she began, "Make my brother well." Such a boon would require a sacrifice. "If you make my brother well, I will dedicate myself to you. I will enter the monastery. I will pray to you and make all honor to you." Sliding the knife from her belt, she said, "Here is the seal on my promise." She nicked the palm of her hand, letting drops of blood fall to the floor in front of the altar. The air shivered. Shagreeta's cat-mouth smiled as if she agreed to the bargain.

Keldara raced back into the house to Keldak's sleeping room. No sound. Mother was smiling. "Shh, he sleeps quietly."

Two days later, Keldak was demanding to get up. That night, Keldara told Mother and Father of her promise to Shagreeta. Mother's hand went to her chest. "No. I can't let you go."

Her father argued, "A promise made by a child is not binding."

"The monastery is far away. We'd be able to visit you only rarely."

"You wouldn't like monastery life." His eyes went around the room, to the floor soft with fleeces, to the ceramic heater, the deep cushions. "There would be no comforts."

"You can worship Shagreeta here at home."

But Keldara was stubborn as stone. "I promised. I promised, and Shagreeta healed Keldak." They knew her narrowed eyes, the uncompromising set of her back. At last her father agreed to accompany her, bringing five goats as a monastery gift.

As she said good-bye to her mother, Keldara sniffed back tears. As she said goodbye to her brother, she hugged him fiercely. His shirt and hers smelled of the herbs her mother put in their clothes press, and she couldn't tell where his scent left off and hers began. Then she began to cry and turned to leave, telling herself she belonged to Shagreeta now.

The journey up the mountain passed in a blur of walking and climbing and prayer as Keldara prayed to Shagreeta at dawn and dusk. Her father asked, "Don't you get tired of praying?"

"Oh no, I like it. It puts joy in my legs. It puts ease in my heart."

At night they usually found a pilgrim inn that offered plain food and a sleeping room shared by all the pilgrims. But the pilgrims often told stories and made music on pipes and drums. The first time Keldara felt shy, but when she saw the innkeeper, she asked what was wrong with his hand. He had cut it, he said, a couple of days ago. She demanded hot water and opened her bag. The other pilgrims glanced at each other, amused by the girl's orders. But she cleaned the wound and put in a couple of stitches with a fine needle, rubbed salve into it, then tied a neat white bandage over it. The innkeeper said, "You're a handy little thing."

They were nearly three weeks on the road. One day they came to the top of a ridge and caught sight of the monastery. Through a haze of mist, tier upon tier of buildings climbed the mountain. Some buildings were bare, honey-colored stone, and others were built of wood painted magenta, jade, and turquoise. Keldara lifted her face to it, consumed with excitement and delight.

The steep path brought them to the entrance. The gate stood open, and a boy in undyed wool robes greeted them. Keldara peered past him. It seemed like hundreds of people were coming and going across the courtyard, and suddenly she wished she were invisible. The boy rang a bell to announce the visitors. A girl came out to take charge of the goats, and an elderly monk in red robes shuffled out to greet them and invite them into his solar.

He moved slowly and stiffly as he prepared hot tea for them over a brazier. "I am Elder Monk. They say I am in charge here, but I mostly do what others tell me to." His cheeks puffed out in good humor.

The tea had an unfamiliar smoky flavor, but Keldara liked it. She curled her fingers around the cup as her father spoke of Keldara's desire to join the monastery. "She doesn't understand no," he warned.

The monk turned to Keldara. She said, "I promised Shagreeta Leopard Goddess that if she spared my brother's life, I would join the monastery and give her my devotion. She agreed. Keldak stopped coughing. He is well now. So I must perform my part of the bargain."

"It is not an easy life, child. Only two or three aspirants join us each year."

"I don't care." It was so clear to her. "I have to do it. I will do it."

He held her hand for a long moment between his two hands like dry, fragile leaves before speaking. "We accept you. I bid you welcome."

He showed Keldara to a room with cold stone walls, a thick woven mat on the floor piled with blankets, and a chest for clothing and personal belongings.

Keldara's father stayed a couple nights in a monastery guest room, resting before making the long journey home. At the gate, he looked at the sky, then at the ground. "Kel, girl," he started, then cleared his throat. "If you want to come home with me…"

Keldara threw her arms around him. "No! No! I must stay." She watched him until the trail curved, and he walked out of sight.

At first, Keldara was homesick. She missed home, her parents, her brother, the house servant, the herders, the farm animals. She missed special dishes the house servant would prepare. The cozy evenings spent listening to stories and mending clothing or doing other tasks. Soon, however, she was too busy to think much about home.

There were hours of instruction in sacred texts. She read and re-read them, trying to learn them so she could serve the deities better.

There was a rhythm of observances—daily, weekly, monthly, and yearly, each with songs and readings, blessings, and rituals.

The monastery taught that the deities existed on prayers and other devotions, and she delighted to think she was feeding Shagreeta. When she prayed, she wore her voice to a thread, yearning for a stronger throat, as she filled with a burning love for the goddess.

One of her favorite devotions was ringing a prayer bell to bring the gods' attention to the invocations inscribed on the metal curve. More than once she stayed behind when the other aspirants had left, ringing so long and so hard that her fingers had to be pried from the handle. Teacher Monk would tell her, "Moderation, moderation," as he massaged her fingers.

There were work duties; everyone was expected to contribute to running the monastery. Keldara was the only aspirant allowed to tend the sick or injured because of her experience and her tenderness with them. She liked healing. But she didn't mind the other chores: shaping the moon candles the monastery sold to pilgrims, peeling and chopping vegetables for soup alongside Cook and the other helpers, sweeping the courtyard.

Sometimes Keldara took on Banyo's chores. He was one of two boys who had joined the monastery earlier in the year. He came from the hot southern lowlands, and the cold and altitude often made him dizzy and nauseated. But he never allowed her to perform his devotions for him, saying, in his foreign grammar, "Respects these are I give to gods. If you do, I do not."

The other boy, Jarathoram, was attractive with dark hair curling around plump cheeks. When he saw that Keldara was doing some of Banyo's chores, he said he was sick and asked if she would take his place helping to prepare the noon meal. She agreed. When he came to eat, looking rested and healthy, she was so angry she flung his bowl of broth and barley at him. "You're sick all right. Sick with laziness." He gaped at her, then down at the mess on his robes as she stalked away.

She went to Elder Monk to confess to her rude behavior. "Elder, I lost my temper."

He seemed to know about it already. He sighed. "You have to control yourself."

"I don't mind doing chores," she mumbled, "I just don't like being made a fool."

"I don't know how to punish you. Shall I forbid your devotions for a week?"

She snapped straight. "You can't do that!" Then Keldara saw that his eyes were twinkling.

He gave her the duty of bringing hot spiced tea to the walled monks. Most aspirants found these monks disturbing. Jara called them creepy. Once they chose to be walled into their solitary cells, the monks spent their remaining days in meditation and prayer. Eventually, they would dry up and stop breathing, and their spirits would ring the iron bell in the courtyard to signal their ascension.

Currently there were five of these monks, in a row of cells away from the bustle of the outer courtyard and refectory. When Keldara brought them tea, they might take the cup through the wall's narrow opening with a smile or remain oblivious, swaying as she set the cup on the ledge, careful not to make a sound. She yearned to be one of them, worshipping Shagreeta with each breath, filled with rapture.

The four years of her aspiration slid by. Her father, mother, and brother came to visit once, a visit long anticipated and over too soon. They prospered; they grew plumper, and their clothing was heavy with embroidery. At first she felt shy of her brother, but he grinned and punched her lightly on the shoulder and called her beanpole, and she punched him back and called him big ox, and then they were easy with each other.

Her mother tried to persuade her to come home. "You've honored Shagreeta enough. Wouldn't you be happier at home?"

"Here is where I belong."

When Keldara was sixteen, the time came for the Choosing ceremony. Each aspirant would be selected by a god or goddess as a devotee, and then the devotee could take First Vows in preparation for Final Vows.

Keldara, Banyo, and Jara, accompanied by the ten high monks, walked through the inner courtyard to the chapel. They filed in, each one touching the silver hand as they passed. Silently Keldara repeated, "Choose me, Shagreeta Leopard, Choose me." Surely Shagreeta would Choose her, after all of her worship. Surely.

A few windows slitted the top of the walls. Most of the light came from lamps filled with sweet oil. They burned from ledges all around the room, a hundred yellow eyes. The air was heavy with the scent of the oil mingled with the fragrance of the flowers strewn in front of the altar.

Brightly colored clay representations of minor gods and goddesses, just a few inches tall, clustered on top of the altar. Glossy black statues of the four high divinities stood on plinths to either side. On the left, Sendo Iron Eagle the Just and Aruna Snow Dove the Merciful. To the right, Khelet Otter, god of good fellowship and laughter, and Shagreeta Leopard. Each seemed to move and breathe in the flickering lamp light. The three aspirants stood in front of the altar, heads bowed. Behind them, the monks lined up in a rustling of robes, a scraping of sandal leather on stone.

Breathily, Elder Monk invoked the deities. His voice strengthened as he asked for their blessing. The room filled with a sense of presence, of attention focused on this one space, this one time. "We have brought you aspirants who yearn to dedicate themselves to your service." Shagreeta's cat-mouth seemed to smile at Keldara.

The monk God's Eye shuffled forward. He was ancient, and so frail that a younger monk had to help lower him into a sitting position on one side of the altar, facing the aspirants and monks. From the folds of his robes he drew the divining sticks—six wands of wood as long as Keldara's forearm, each with four sides carved with pictographs. He gestured to Banyo.

Banyo came forward and knelt, shivering a little, looking even thinner and paler than usual. God's Eye tossed the sticks straight up into the air, where they hung and spun for several moments before tumbling to the floor. A shudder went through Banyo's body. God's Eye leaned forward to examine the pictographs and the pattern the sticks made.

He announced, "Khelet Otter God Chooses Aspirant Banyo." Keldara was surprised that the god of laughter and good fellowship had chosen the most serious aspirant.

Banyo rose and smiled as Elder Monk embraced him.

Next, Jara was gestured forward. He knelt but folded the bottom of his underrobe to pad his knees. God's Eye threw the sticks. Again they hung and spun, then rattled on the floor. God's Eye read them silently, taking a few minutes, then threw them again. They spun briefly, then descended in the same pattern as before, with the same sides uppermost.

God's Eye spoke. "No god, no goddess chooses Jarathoram."

Jara's face flushed red. "Throw them again."

"Certainly." God's Eye threw them again. "The same."

"Again."

God's Eye threw them again and again, always with the same outcome.

Finally Elder Monk bent over and put a hand on Jara's shoulder. "Enough. Come. You may stay here as a lay brother, you know. Or we will give you a little money and clothing, and you can make your way in the world." Jara lurched to his feet, and Elder Monk guided him to one side.

God's Eye gestured to Keldara. She threw herself on her knees before the altar and bowed her head, then leaned over, pressing her forehead to the cold rough stone. Her heart was pounding so hard she couldn't breathe. Shagreeta would choose her, wouldn't she? The sticks tumbled on the floor. A huge paw came to rest on her shoulder, heavy velvet, claws sheathed. "Serve me." The words vibrated. Keldara's body shuddered.

"Shagreeta Leopard Goddess Chooses Aspirant Keldara."

That night the monastery feasted, and Keldara and Banyo in yellow devotee robes sat at the monks' table and were served by aspirants. Jara didn't appear.

The next morning Keldara and Banyo were each given a few coins and some food and water. Elder Monk stood at the gate to say farewell. "You must go out and learn about the world. You may return with skills we can use. Or you may find that you want to stay in the world, that you do not wish to take Final Vows."

"But I already know," argued Keldara. "I know I want to stay, to take the vows." She had told him this before. The argument hadn't worked before, and it didn't work now.

"For you to go is good. It is right. It is necessary."

Keldara bowed to Elder Monk and strode away, impatient to get the year done and return to worship Shagreeta.

The year passed. The aspirant at the gate was new. He bowed out of respect for her yellow robes, but she just nodded at him as she passed. She needed to see Shagreeta.

She went directly into the inner courtyard and stopped in front of the iron door. Taking a deep breath, she touched the silver hand and opened the door.

The chapel was dim, with only a few sweet-oil lamps burning. The minor deities in their bright colors still stood on the altar. The high deities rested black and glossy on their plinths.

Keldara walked over to Shagreeta and knelt, but instead of bowing her head, she looked up into the cat-face.

Her voice rasped. "I went home, wanting to see my family. The plague had come before me. Mother and Father were dead, swelling and rotting. My brother begged me to ease his thirst even as I held the cup to his mouth. He died as I held him."

Silence.

"I didn't know what to do, so I traveled. I saw men with sores all over their bodies. Women with bruises and fevers. Children who hungered and died. A valley of dead and dying soldiers, plucked at by vultures." Words caught in her throat. She continued in a whisper. "Why do You allow it? Why don't You heal them?"

Silence.

Keldara's hands clenched, and her voice rose. "I rang the prayer bell for You. I made ten thousand prayers to You. I would have drained my veins for You."

Silence.

Keldara took out her knife and ran it across her palm. Blood welled up. She smeared it across the black stone mouth. "I'm done with You."

Keldara journeyed to the lowlands. She sought out a healer, one who was spoken of with respect and affection. Although he had never before taken an apprentice, she attached herself to him, following him and asking questions, until he finally took her on. When he died, people came to her with their injuries and illnesses.

Late one evening, when she had found time to relax at home, a monk in red robes came to the door. Laugh lines radiated from his eyes and cheeks. "Know you me?"

"Banyo!" She was so happy to see him that she grasped his forearms hard, and he squeezed her arms back. They sat up all night drinking tea and talking.

Banyo had taken Final Vows and had chosen to be an itinerant monk. As he walked all over, he greeted everyone he met with words of encouragement or a joke. "I like to see their shoulders untense, their faces relax into smiles. I like to leave behind harmony and kindness."

His smile faded, and he leaned forward. "A plea for help I bring. Plague has come to the high valleys of the northern mountains. Villagers beg you to come, healer Keldara, beloved Keldara."

"Healer Keldara. Beloved Keldara. I don't know where those come from. You'd think I was a saint."

He chuckled.

Keldara journeyed to the mountains and went from community to community. As she went, she imparted knowledge of treatments and remedies, and she learned from local healers.

And now she found herself on the ridge below the monastery. Twenty years had passed since she and her father had looked up and seen the tiers of buildings through the misty air. She remembered her excitement, her delight.

She leaned on her staff of golden wood that was carved with images of healing—sick people rising from their beds, hearts knitting together, legs straightening. It had been a gratitude gift from a master woodcarver whose son she had saved. She often received gifts, and she was always deeply appreciative, even if she gave them away. This one had served her well, supporting her for miles and miles. It supported her now as she pondered.

She decided she wanted to see the monastery again. Wanted to see Shagreeta again.

The aspirant at the gate asked how he could direct her, glancing between her plain woolen wrap and the ornate staff.

"I suppose I am a pilgrim of sorts." He bowed. "Please be welcome. I will call someone to help you."

"No need."

Although so many years had passed, her feet still remembered the curve of stones through her felt shoes. Her ears still knew the ringing of the prayer bells. Children stared at her, curious about the stranger. They looked so young, with smooth faces and bright eyes. Good memories of doing her devotions with Banyo and Jara floated up. What had happened to Elder Monk and the others who had taught her and cared for her?

As she entered the inner courtyard, the sound of bells faded, and the mutter of prayers from the meditation cells grew louder. At the chapel door she touched the silver hand and grasped the cold iron handle and stepped inside.

Sweet-oil lamps burning. Minor deities in bright paint. The high deities glossy and black.

Slowly Keldara walked over to face Shagreeta, her staff tapping and echoing. Shagreeta's cat-mouth smiled.

Leaning on the staff, Keldara pondered what to say. She straightened. Her voice was clear and strong. "I learned to treat the ones You ignored. I treated rich folk for coin but poor folk for free. Lepers and plague victims sought me out; I turned no one away."

She remembered the tumbling of the divining sticks, could almost hear them rattle on the floor. Felt the paw, heavy on her shoulder. She had been so happy, sure that she would always worship Shagreeta, be on fire with divine radiance. She heard Shagreeta's voice again, echoing as if through a vast distance. "Serve me."

Keldara's fingers traced the carvings on the staff, signifiers of what she had accomplished.

Shagreeta's voice. "Serve me." Not "Worship me." Shagreeta did not want a worshipper lost in her own rapture. She wanted a healer. Someone to treat the ones she herself could not help.

Keldara's throat tightened. Her eyes blurred with hot tears. She threw herself on her knees in front of Shagreeta, Shagreeta in gray fur with dark rosettes, Shagreeta with amber eyes and cat-mouth smile.

A tongue touched her cheek. Words purred. "Daughter. My daughter."

Risk

You can try
hiding in the hut
with the cold fireplace
and empty table.

Sometimes
you have to leave the path
and let the crows eat the breadcrumbs.
You have to risk the witches.

Sacrifice

The goddess manifested but once a year, to grant petitions and to take the sacrifice. Now, perched on the divine throne, her chitinous legs tapping the twisted silver strands, she gazed at the preparations with one multi-faceted eye, then the other. One of her priests moved around the shrine lighting the lamps. The flames' reflections shivered in the slick black marble walls. Other priests filled blue-glazed bowls with water and floated flowers in them. She approved of their quiet, respectful movements, their bowed heads.

When the preparations were completed, they slowly pushed open the double bronze doors twice their height, so heavy the priests had to lean into them.

Eight supplicants had gathered in the outer courtyard and had been dressed in clean white linen robes. The year before, only one had dared to make a petition.

She would take only one to be the sacrifice, but all who offered themselves would have their petitions fulfilled, simply because they were willing to hazard their lives.

When the doors were open and the prayer-bells shaken, priests shepherded the supplicants into the shrine. Some stumbled on fear-frozen legs; others sagged and could hardly walk at all. They stopped partway to the throne, huddled together as if for safety.

The priests began their prayer-chants. The goddess hungered, and she moved restlessly. When the prayers ended, she descended from the throne, first the head and heavy, serrated forelegs, then the twiggy middle and back legs.

She stalked toward the supplicants, who leaned away from her, trembling. Their sweat stank of fear. Tears slipped down one woman's face, but she didn't seem to notice them, eyes wide and staring at the goddess. The supplicants didn't look at each other; all their attention was pinned on the goddess.

Most wore a bag on a flax cord around their neck, stuffed with thin paper closely written with prayers for safety and deliverance, and the bags rose and fell with their jagged breathing. Amused, the goddess noted that one man wore a moonstone carved with the head of the falcon god, to ward away evil. A woman had rubbed her body with bitter-smelling herbs, hoping to make herself unappealing. A thickset man had decorated his arms and legs with henna, interweaving signs for good fortune—pointed waves signifying the mother river, the turtle for long life, folded hands for supplication. A man's lips were moving soundlessly, but the goddess read, "Don't take me, don't take me, don't take me." That was what they all wished, of course, that their prayer would be granted, but that she would take someone else.

The man who had petitioned alone last year had worn no prayer bag, no amulets or decorations. His face had been pale as clay, and his breath had come in gasps, but his steps were firm as they took him to her throne.

Now, as she circled the eight supplicants, the goddess descried their petitions in their minds: for generous crops after three years of barren fields to keep the family from starving; for the sickness in the lungs to be healed so he could live a long life; for a husband to be brought home safely from battle; for a healthy baby, not one that struggled its way out of the womb only to sicken and die.

The man with the amulet dashed for the doorway, tripped with his own speed, and fell sprawling on the marble floor, then scuttled out on hands and feet. No one tried to stop him. His petition would go unfulfilled.

The goddess paused in front of a woman whose legs gave way; she sank to the floor, covering her face with her hands. Lust and jealousy boiled in her. She wanted her friend to die so that she could have the husband. The goddess's jaw clicked sideways, and she hissed, "Take her away." Two priests hauled her to her feet and led her out between the bronze doors. Her petition would go unfulfilled.

Only six remained. Each darted glances at the others, realizing their odds had just narrowed.

Any one of them would make a suitable sacrifice, and she was hungry. Her two front legs shot out and seized the thickset man. A choked, thin whimper. Her mandibles crunched through the neck. The body went limp and heavy as she dragged it to the throne for her goddess-meal.

The year before, the lone supplicant had knelt in front of her throne and bowed his head, baring the nape of his neck. Slowly, reluctantly, she had descended from the throne to inspect him.

There are imperatives even a goddess must obey. Finally she had hissed, "Your son will be well," before accepting his life. But she tasted no flesh and lapped no blood. Instead, she had turned away and told the priests, "Take the body to his family."

Juliet (Mannequin on Balcony)

You can see the mileage on my skin.
My head bald as the day I was made—
eyeless, armless.

I know Romeo is not
going to stand below
and praise the brightness
of my eyes, call me
the sun—
maybe the moon,
with her pale, scarred face.

Still, the day is warm
and I can watch the passersby
strolling on two legs,
gesturing with two hands.
Men glancing at women
and their two soft breasts.
Eating, talking,
laughing, kissing.

Unharnessed

As she left the oncologist's office, Eileen felt shaky and almost sick, blinking in the sharp sunlight. Dazed, she stumbled to the bus stop.

Why hadn't she used her breasts more? Let the high school boys touch them? Let them out of their cups and straps to let them swing in front of the lovers she had never had? Let them fill with milk for the baby that had never had a chance to be conceived? Touched them herself in gratitude?

Eileen collapsed onto the bus stop bench. "I won't cry. I won't."

At the other end of the bench a girl, maybe in her late teens, was hunched over, counting coins in her palm. She gave off an... odor. Her breasts shifted, loose beneath the stained t-shirt.

The girl's face was long and pale, her coarse hair bleached white, a forelock almost obscuring a mark on her forehead, a golden spiral that curled around itself, almost glowing. Kids and their tattoos. But this tattoo was pretty. Strange that it was in the middle of her forehead.

The girl counted her coins again. She snuffled, nostrils quivering. Slumped at her feet was a black plastic garbage bag. Was that all the girl owned?

Eileen fumbled in her purse for her wallet, careful not to pull it out too far. She held out two $20s. The girl startled, tossing up her head, then took the money in a grubby hand.

"Thank you, ma'am. Appreciate it." Her voice was hoarse and high-pitched, slightly accented. She stared at Eileen's face, then dropped her gaze to Eileen's breasts. Eileen shifted uncomfortably and was about to stand when the girl closed her eyes and leaned over, pressing her forehead against Eileen's left breast, then the right. Eileen jumped back so fast her head slapped against the shelter's post. "What the—?" Her breasts tingled. A warmth spread through her chest.

The girl drew back. "I'm a unicorn," she whispered. "My horn is magical, just like in the tales."

The girl was crazy. Eileen scrambled to her feet. "I have to..."

The girl looked away, then slanted her eyes back to Eileen. "It would be better if I nuzzled them. We could go somewhere, and I could do the job proper."

The hairs stood up on Eileen's arms. Words jammed in her throat. She opened her mouth, closed it. Breath held. Hand to her chest.

The Woman Who Lived by the Ocean
Was Lonely and Tried to Make Herself a Husband

She took
a thread of wind, a shred of weed
longing and wildness
3-arrowed runes in the sand
the beating of a gull's heart, *skitter-kik, skitter-kik*
quick pulse of seawater
2 dark tears
white light of dawn.

When she finished,
it uttered no words but a cry,
trembled on the wind,
and flew away,
away over the green wave.

Pretty Butterfly

Shiraz led Angel up the steps to the wraparound porch and big, solid-looking doors. The doors parted, and an elderly woman hobbled onto the porch. Angel stared at the silver-knobbed cane. Couldn't she be blueprinted to fix her leg? Angel wanted to cry, as she had cried over the lame alley cat she had caught and taken to the vet.

"What's this?" The sweep of the hand included Angel, Shiraz, and the carrycase.

"Hi, Aunt Agatha. This is my daughter, Angel. Your great-niece. Remember? You sent her a lovely christening present."

"And now she's come to thank me for it?" Aunt Agatha barked a laugh. "About time. How many years has it been? Six? Seven?"

"She's 10 now." Shiraz paused. "You got the card I cybercast? I'm getting married. Maurizio and I are planning a ceremony and honeymoon in the LaGrange spa—you know, the one in orbit."

"And a child would be all in your way." Aunt Agatha snorted and banged her cane on the porch floor. "Didn't occur to you to ask if a child would be all in my way, eh?"

Shiraz said, "Since you never had children of your own, I thought it would be fun for you."

"Doing me a favor. I see." Aunt Agatha peered at Angel, her lens implants catching the light. "Quiet, isn't she? Not like you. What's that on her back? Wings? Good heavens. Pun intended." Her laugh barked out again.

Angel's face got warm, and her wings twitched.

"Sorry, I shouldn't have said that. You make a remark about my ancient, wobbly leg. All right?"

Angel gave a tiny shake of her head no. Shiraz straightened the wings where they emerged from slits in Angel's top and smoothed the feathers. "Yes, I had her blueprinted. I thought little fluttery angel wings would be so cute. And creative. All my friends said I was so creative. But it turned out they can't gen-eng wings—I don't know why—so there was the cost of the surgery, and then there was the blond hair and blue eyes on top of that." She sighed.

"We'll be back in two or three weeks. She's really an angel. Won't cause you any trouble." With a kiss on top of Angel's head and one in the vicinity of Aunt Agatha's cheek, she whisked away.

Aunt Agatha said, "Well," and tapped her cane. "You'd better grab the carrycase." She used the cane to punch a button on the wall, and the doors parted. As she hobbled inside, Angel caught her violet scent. It was light and sweet.

A week went by. Shiraz sent a video from the LaGrange space station. She looked beautiful in a flower-print sarong, feet floating off the floor. "We just got married. We miss you." Maurizio started flapping his arms and bouncing slowly like a balloon. Shiraz gave him a peeved look, then turned her face back to the camera. "Back soon. Be good."

Two weeks. No word.

Three weeks. Aunt Agatha told Angel that honeymoons were busy times.

Two months later Shiraz fluttered in with no warning, hanging on Maurizio's arm and handing out gifts of crystals grown in space and 3D photos from Hubble 2, and telling tales of their adventures. Maurizio smiled and nodded in all the right places.

After a couple of hours Shiraz asked Aunt Agatha if they could talk in private, and they disappeared into the sitting room.

Angel had only met Maurizio a couple of times, and only with Shiraz. She didn't really know him.

He cleared his throat. "How do you like school?"

"I'm distance learning. Sometimes I have a tutor."

"Don't you want to go to school and have fun with the other kids?"

Angel didn't know what to say. Silence. Finally, "So you're going to be my stepdad."

He looked startled. "That's right. I hadn't really thought of it like that." Reaching into a pocket, he took out a credit chip. "Since you're now my stepdaughter—my favorite stepdaughter—"

Angel giggled. "Your only stepdaughter."

"—hush, I'm making a speech."

Angel giggled again.

"I have to give you money. That's what stepdads are for."

"But—"

"Really." He laid the chip in her hand.

"Thank you. You…"

Shiraz bustled in, followed by Aunt Agatha. Then everything happened so fast. Angel was kissed good-bye, and Shiraz and Maurizio were gone, with no mention of taking Angel with them. But eventually someone would tell her what the plans were for her.

That evening Angel set the small table where they usually ate their meals—the kitchen windows let in a lot of light—and dialed up supper. The conveyor made its usual creaking noises as it transferred the meal packs from storage into the heating and cooling compartments.

Aunt Agatha picked up a fork. "That meal system sounds like it'll break down any minute now. I'm going to have to hire someone to come look at it."

Did Aunt Agatha need money? Angel reached out the credit chip. "Maurizio gave me this. I don't know if it would pay for a technician."

"Oh, darling. No, no, keep it. I have pots of money. Your mother knows. Ha!" She fiddled with the fork, set it down again.

"Here are your choices. You can go to a boarding school, you can stay with me and do distance learning, or you can stay with me and go to the public school. It's not fancy, but it gives a good, basic education."

No mention of living with Shiraz and Maurizio. They didn't want her. Angel's stomach twisted. She stared down at her plate and struggled to put on her obedient face. "Whatever you want."

"It's your choice."

"I want to stay with you. If that's all right. And—" she remembered what Maurizio had said about having fun with other kids. "I want to go to public school."

After supper Aunt Agatha took Angel to her room and opened her jewelry chest. She selected a gold ring with swirls like hands holding a blue stone and handed it to Angel. "It's old-fashioned, I know."

"It's for me? To keep?"

Aunt Agatha shaped the memory-metal band until it fit snugly on Angel's finger. "Yes, for you to keep." She sat back on her recliner, sighing as she tried to find a comfortable position.

"Thank you! So very, very much!" Angel stroked the stone as she looked at the shine and sparkle of the other pieces. "What beautiful things you have!" She picked up a cameo brooch. "I've never seen you wear this." She pinned it on Aunt Agatha's dress. Giggling, she slid heavy jeweled rings onto wrinkled fingers, pinned on brooches at random, draped gold chains around her aunt's neck. Standing back to contemplate her work, she said, "You look like a queen."

"Queen of the Aged, maybe."

Angel sighed. "Shiraz would love these."

"Yes, your mother loves expensive, pretty things. And I was going to leave them to her. But they'll be yours when I'm gone."

"But you won't be gone for a long, long time."

School was crowded and noisy, and there was a weird smell of cleaning chemicals. Her wings kept twitching. Kids walking by stared at her. "New girl." "Look, she has wings." "Hey, do you play the harp?" One boy tugged on them as he went by, then ran after his friends. "They're real." Angel could feel her face burning.

Eventually she found the principal's office and went in. A middle-aged woman with soft cheeks greeted her. "You must be Angel."

"Yes. My aunt couldn't make it. Her leg is bad today."

Angel answered questions, and the woman keyed data into the computer and handed her a tablet. "Here's your schedule and a map and some information about the school. I'll take you to your first class. Um, is there any way you can tuck your wings inside your sweater?" The woman tried to fold them inside the slits so they would rest against her back. "Oh dear. They don't really fit. Well, you put on a smile, and we'll go in."

By the end of the day Angel was exhausted and longed to go home. When the bell rang the other kids trooped out of the classroom, but the teacher gestured for her to come up front.

He sat on the edge of the desk, swinging a leg. "The other kids aren't used to blueprinting. The families around here mostly can't afford it, and when they get it, it's for intelligence or sports abilities, not for, um, cosmetic reasons. But they'll get used to you. By next week you won't be a celebrity anymore. So give it a week, okay?"

"Okay," she whispered. All she wanted was to fit in.

When she got home, Aunt Agatha asked how her first day had gone.

"Fine."

"Did the other kids tease you about the wings?"

Angel's smile faded. "Yes. But the teacher said they would get used to them."

"Would you like to hide them?"

"Oh yes."

The next day they went to Aunt Agatha's dressmaker, who measured Angel with a cloth tape instead of lasers, and arranged to have cotton tops ready in a week. The tops were cut full in the back so she could tuck her wings in. It helped with the staring and whispers.

One day that summer it was so hot she wore one of her old blouses and pulled the wings through the slits. As she was going through a revolving door, a wing got caught and was torn so badly Aunt Agatha took her to quick care. While the nurse was stitching it up, Aunt Agatha said, "Your wings are pretty, but they seem to get in the way. Do you want them removed?"

Tears of pain in her eyes, Angel shook her head. Her mother had had her blueprinted this way.

A few weeks later Shiraz swept in unannounced with gifts and a new boyfriend. When the new boyfriend left the room to go to the toilet, Angel asked, "What happened to Maurizio? I liked him."

Shiraz hunched a shoulder. "He was a 49er."

"A 49er?"

"Digging for gold." She blinked for a moment as if holding back tears, then said, "How do you like my latest blueprinting?"

"I like the eyelashes. The tiger stripes are… colorful."

In the following years, Shiraz would appear unexpectedly, each time with gifts and a new boyfriend. There would be a few hours of laughing and joking, and then she would leave.

Aunt Agatha said, "She does liven things up."

Shiraz came to Angel's high school graduation. Angel's friends asked who that was sitting with her aunt and said how young and thin she looked. Angel smiled as she memorized the compliments to pass on to Shiraz. Aunt Agatha thumped her cane as Angel went up to the front to receive her diploma.

Two weeks later, Aunt Agatha died. Her heart had been bad for years. When Angel went to call her for breakfast, she was lying in bed as still as a doll, a hint of violet scent lingering in the air.

From then on, everything was jumbled. Calling an ambulance. Being told there was nothing they could do. Leaving a message for Shiraz. Talking with the funeral director, who was kind and helpful. Calling friends and relatives. Arranging a lunch at home for after the service. Angel's throat felt raw with weeping.

At the funeral service she watched for her mother, although Shiraz had often confessed to a horror of funerals due to her extreme sensitivity.

When Angel arrived back at the house, the caterer was setting out food, and two beverage carts were roaming the front rooms in a random pattern around the heavy furniture.

Surely Shiraz would come to the lunch. The rooms filled up with people, and Angel spoke with distant relatives, her friends and their parents, and townspeople Aunt Agatha had done business with. It was getting to be evening, and the caterer was packing up by the time she spotted Shiraz. She recognized her mother not by her face but by her laugh tinkling across the dining room as she responded to something the lawyer said. Shiraz's slanted eyes gleamed green. Locks of silvery-white hair squiggled down her forehead, set off by caramel-colored skin. She looked fairylike and fragile. As Angel came nearer, she saw that Shiraz's bones pressed against the skin. Her velvet dress sagged where her breasts should have plumped it out and drooped at her hips where it should have swirled.

Shiraz tossed her head, the laugh gone. Hunching a shoulder at the lawyer, she moved away. Angel hurried to greet her.

Shiraz kissed Angel's cheek and put her arms around her. One hand traced the curve of a wing. "So pretty and soft. I'm so creative."

"And now—" her mother frowned, and she looked as if she were trying to think of something but finally gave up. "I need a drink."

Quickly, Angel said, "I'll get you a glass of shiraz." She poured from the beverage cart.

"Thank you, Angel. You're an angel." Her mother held the glass up to her nose, breathing in the scent. "But I'm not Shiraz anymore, I changed my name." She poured half of the wine down her throat.

"What did you change it to?"

Her mother threw Angel a playful look. "What do you think?"

"You look like a fairy sprite."

Her mother smiled and patted a silver curl. "I'm Titania. The fairy queen."

"How pretty."

"Yes. And creative. All my friends say so." She gulped the rest of the wine, then stared at the bottom of the empty glass. "You're the age I was when I blueprinted you. My parents had both died in that car crash. I wanted someone who would love me."

Angel's mouth opened, but she didn't know what her mother wanted to hear. *I do love you? I'm sorry?*

Her mother hunched a shoulder again and slammed the glass down on the nearest table. "So everything goes to you. You're only a great-niece. I'm her niece. She must have gone senile."

"No, her mind was all there. She made bequests. She left you some money, and cousin Rose, and charities…"

"She left me a drop. And apparently I can't even get my drop until the will is proved, or something, and heaven knows when that will be. That lawyer is an idiot. He certainly wasn't blueprinted for brains." Muttering, Titania stalked off.

Eventually everyone left. The lawyer said good-bye and told her to call him if she needed anything. The caterer disappeared with his carts. Her mother must have left without saying good-bye. She had never liked saying good-bye.

The rooms felt cold. Angel wiped her eyes. Maybe she would feel better among her aunt's things. She trudged to the back and parted the doors.

Her mother was leaning over the jewelry cabinet. Its lid was up, and drawers were pulled out. A handbag sat on the floor, gaping open, a strand of moonstones slithering down its side.

At the sound of the door, her mother started, and her head jerked up. Angel stood rigid in the doorway. For a long minute they stared at each other. Finally Angel croaked out, "What are you doing?"

A spot of color burned in each caramel cheek, turning them a grayish color. Titania began, "I was just—I—" Her eyes blinked too fast. Finally she tossed her head. "A drop, that's all she left me. And I need money for—for something important, I can't tell you what."

Angel's stomach burned, and her mouth felt dry. "They're mine now. The house and everything in it are mine."

A trace of violet scent touched Angel's nostrils. Jewels couldn't take Aunt Agatha's place. Whatever they would buy couldn't take Aunt Agatha's place. Tears rose in Angel's throat. "It's all right," she said gently, as if comforting a child. "Take what you want."

Titania grabbed a handful of rings and stuffed them in her bag, spilling some on the floor. Without bothering to pick them up, she stumbled out of the room, footsteps thumping down the hall until the door slammed.

Angel's arms and legs folded beneath her like a marionette whose strings had been cut, and she collapsed on the recliner. Her wings pinched, and she reached over her shoulder to free them. Tomorrow she would call a surgeon to have them removed.

An Unlooked-for Moment of Grace

today
you stand in the sun
and happiness pours into you

mending the broken places
filling every chip and rift with gold

Warrior

Annika leaned forward, eyes narrowed, watching the holovideo recording of last year's Blood Ring fight. Liess and Marga had drawn their longknives and were circling each other.

Annika's father had recorded commentary for Annika. "Liess uses both hands, but you have a half-inch reach on her." Pause. "Marga lost the fight the minute she had armor plates inserted under the skin of her belly. It's a defense move." Liess's longknife flashed. Marga took a shallow slash to her ribs and backed away. "See? Not aggressive enough. She was quicker and stronger than Liess, but Liess is fierce. You'll have to lay her out on the canvas to win. Remember. There's no room for softness in the Blood Ring." It was part of the Norder culture, and something her father had told her again and again. Be aggressive. Throw away caution.

She had been training with her father for 10 years. On her fourteenth birthday, after the age ceremony, he sat her down at the eating table. She still remembered her stomach heavy with sweets, the half-empty cup on the table next to her, and the scent of honeyed wine. He said, "You're strong and you're fast and you're smart. You have what it takes to be Blood Ring champion." His eyes moved to his jeweled belt in its glass case, then back to her face. "I can train you. Are you willing to work so hard your blood is bursting your eyes and ears, and your muscles are on their last twitch, and your body is bruised black and blue?"

She had just returned from several months of mandatory field training with her age cohort, learning how to fight in different terrains—temperate forest, a jungle, desert, mountains, snowy tundra. She had loved them all. In fact, she was thinking of becoming a field instructor.

But now this. Didn't everyone aspire to be Blood Ring champion? And her father would be training her. She couldn't speak, she was so overcome with pride and excitement, but her head bobbed up and down.

He had been behind her as she worked her way up from Brass Ring to Silver Ring to Gold Ring. And now to Blood Ring, the highest level.

Then the Norder Council had decided to move the entire colony to another planet. The new home was closer to a major galactic transit hub, so they could pursue more mercenary contracts, and mercenaries could visit home more often. There would be better access to up-to-date technologies for weapons and medical care.

They had to hire a ship to make the move. It was owned and staffed by marinheiros, a culture that specialized in transport and trade. The trip would take two and a half years with three wormhole jumps. The expense was astronomical.

The Council encouraged her father and some of the other trainers to take lucrative mercenary contracts off-planet to help pay for the move.

She had said good-bye to her father at the space station, where he would get passage to the Elumet star system. He was to help a prince who was defending his territory against a neighboring prince. It didn't seem too dangerous, although there would likely be some border skirmishes. As they stood in the docking area, travelers ebbing and flowing around them, Annika wanted to tell him, you have to stay and train me, advise me, tell me I can win. Instead, she said, "You have to see me become Blood Ring Champion."

"You don't need me. Just make me proud of you."

Now she was in her new quarters on board the marinheiro ship, reviewing holovideo recordings, preparing for the Blood Ring. Only two months away.

A chime sounded. Annika shook her head to clear it. The chime sounded again. "Damnation." Time to go on the ship orientation tour. What a waste of time when she could be studying fights or training.

The room was so cramped she had to swing her legs around in order to mold the seat's memory plastic back into the wall. The bed was a shelf with storage underneath, and she had to turn sideways to get into her bathing and toilet cubicle. Everyone complained that the transport ship was too small.

She got lost going through the corridors to meet the group. All the corridors looked the same, with brushed-metal walls and beige matting on the floors. As she finally joined the other Norders, a group of about 20 adults and a couple of children, the guide was introducing himself. He looked like a typical marinheiro, slim and dark-haired, slighter than the Norders. "I am Lidio da Silva. The da Silva extended family owns the ship and operates it. Most of the crew is connected with the family, although some of the more specialized positions, like pilot, we have to hire outside the family."

Annika felt a little unsteady, like her reflexes were off. The da Silva—what was his first name?—was explaining they would get used to the ship's gravity. "It's about 7/8 what you're used to. The amount of power the gravity system sucks up is unbelievable."

Annika had had training in null-G and in spin, but years ago. She decided to message her father for his advice. In the meantime, she'd switch up her training to focus on virtual reality fights, maybe find someone to spar with until her reflexes adjusted.

The guide said, "We know it's a huge change for you, coming from your home on Greenhame planet. The ship is like an enclosed town. There are about 8,000 Norders, almost your entire clan. And about 2,000 crew—the da Silvas and others—plus our families. This ship is our home. We are born on the ship, many of us. We live our lives on the ship."

Two marinheiros passed the group, going the other way. Annika heard the word "Norders" and turned to look back at them, clenching the right side of her jaw to turn up her hearing augment. "All of the training and fighting and mercenary contracts. And they hired us to take them to where they can fight more conveniently."

"That's how they make money, a lot of them, as mercenaries."

"That's what I'm saying, it's all about the fighting."

Annika turned back to the group. Pointing out a training facility off the hallway, the guide said, "We installed additional workout rooms for you. There is at least one in every sector." Annika peeked in. It was small but had the basic equipment, including a virtual reality cell.

At the end of the corridor the guide stopped and pressed buttons on a console to open the airlock. He waited on the other side for everyone to regroup. The first thing Annika noticed was the air, cool and moist, with plant scents. It smelled alive after the ship's flat air, and she gulped it in as she looked around. There were acres and acres of natural landscaping, with woods, a lake, meadows, a prairie, marshlands, rolling hills. It was disconcerting how the land curved up at the sides, but the sides were so far away they looked hazy.

Annika liked it right away. It reminded her of the months her age cohort had spent field training.

The guide continued, "This is what is officially known as the Ecological Resource Area. We call it the Wild. It occupies much of the space in the center of the ship, along the longitudinal axis, like the core of a fruit."

Some Norders in the group muttered about wasted space, and a limited number of training facilities, and small suite sizes.

The guide explained, "The Wild plays an important role in maintaining the ship's ecology and also provides psychological benefits. You'll be surprised by how hungry you get for green."

One woman asked, "Why is it uphill on the sides?"

"It follows the curve of the ship, the cylinder. But what many people find odd is that when they walk, they don't notice the curve, it's so gradual. Then they look back, and where they came from is on a curve."

A child, maybe 10 years old, asked, "Are there animals?"

"There's some wildlife, miniature deer, for instance, other small mammals, lizards, amphibians, fish, insects. No big predators, no wolves or bears or wildcats." The child looked disappointed. "You'll see some waterbirds. But you won't see birds on the wing. For some reason birds don't fly. Scientists think it might be due to some subtle effect of the gravity system, but no one really knows."

A Norder man. "Why the airlock?"

"In case the hull is breached, each sector can be sealed off to contain its air. The Wild is the largest sector."

When they left, Annika lagged behind and slipped away from the group to retrace the steps to the training room. As she turned a corner, she heard the guide say, "We don't expect any emergencies, but..."

She went into the virtual reality cell and booted up the fight program and pulled out her longknife.

The Blood Ring had been installed last night. It seemed to float in darkness, a 24-foot by 24-foot square of stained canvas lit by spotlights.

No ropes. If you went over the edge, it was a 20-foot plunge down to the deck. The crew had assigned it the largest entertainment area on the ship and had taken out the stage and reconfigured the tiered seating. Still, it only accommodated about 1,000 spectators, and many Norders complained about not being able to watch the most important event of the year. Arrangements had been made for a videocast. Crew members were making last-minute adjustments to the lights and sound equipment. Two marinheiro medics hovered nearby. The audience tiers were filling up.

Annika's father couldn't get away from his contract, but he had said he'd watch the cast.

Annika waited in the holding area across from the Ring. Her blond hair was buzzed to an inch from her scalp, and she was wearing a thin knit top and shorts that outlined her muscles. She pulled her silk-steel gauntlet over her left hand, up her forearm, and over her biceps. Her skin prickled as the nanobots gripped it.

On the other side of the Ring, Liess was wearing much the same outfit, except her light-brown hair was woven into a tight braid and pinned to the back of her head. Annika knew a metal spike was braided inside, a hidden sting. More than once she had seen Liess braid it into her hair prior to a fight.

Liess had been in the year-group ahead of Annika, but everyone knew she was one of the school's best fighters, and that she had flayed off strips of skin to show she could stand the pain. Scars still striped her forearm. Her legs had newer thin white scars where she had had the nerves augmented to make her faster.

Liess's trainer was leaning toward her, whispering, no doubt some last-minute advice. Annika turned up her hearing augment but couldn't make out what he was saying.

What would Annika's father be telling her now? That she had been training all-out and was hard and whip-snap fast. What else? To make sure she was warmed up. She went through the familiar routine of slow, controlled movements, gradually speeding them up. What else would he say? This is the Blood Ring. Don't look for any softness here.

The techs huddled with the referee and then left to stand behind their equipment. The first bell rang. Annika's whole body quivered. Deep breaths. Shoulder rolls. Dip the hands into powder to absorb the sweat. The ritual calmed her a little.

The referee stood in the center of the Ring.

Second bell. She and Liess walked down their catwalks to their corners on opposite sides of the ring, pumping their fists to shouts and whistles from the audience. Annika bent to run her hand over the stained canvas and smell what remained of old blood and sweat.

The catwalks were rolled away.

The referee drew his longknife. Held it up for a long moment. Then threw it down so the point stuck in the canvas and the blade quivered. The crowd exhaled and slapped their chests.

She and Liess drew their longknives at the same moment and stepped toward each other.

Annika saw only Liess, the glint as her longknife caught the light. Heard only the tread of Liess's feet on the canvas, the huff-huff of her breath, the thumping of her heart, strong and steady.

For a few moments she and Liess circled each other, their knives making tiny circles and figure eights. Annika knew to the inch where she was on the Ring and how far away the edge was. She looked at Liess's eyes but watched her chest and hands and feet in her peripheral vision. Liess's eyes narrowed, and she snaked out a foot. Annika lengthened her stride just enough to avoid it. Liess took in a sharp breath, bent her knees, and sprang into the air. One foot kicked out, then the other. Annika turned her hip to take the hits. She shifted knife hands, leaped forward. A roar—Annika didn't know if it was the pounding of her blood or the crowd. Liess sliced down with her longknife. Annika blocked it with her gauntlet. The knife skittered off the silk-steel. Annika rammed her shoulder into Liess's belly. "Unh." Annika's hand shot out and curled around Liess's neck. The windpipe was so alive, slick with sweat, quivering and straining. Liess gasped, a strangled sound. Choking. Dying? Annika didn't mean to loosen her grip. Her fingers eased, just a little.

Canvas bounced off Annika's cheekbone. Liess sliced the longknife down her thigh. Then she pulled out the bloodied knife and pumped it into the air. The roar mounted into a shriek.

Annika pressed a hand to her thigh, blood surging between her fingers. The referee fastened the jeweled belt around Liess's waist, and she made the traditional salutation, slapping her chest in each of the four cardinal directions, then holding her fists above her head.

Only when she was done was a catwalk wheeled to the Ring to allow the medics to treat Annika. One attached a long puffy patch over the wound. He nodded to the other medic, and they slid her onto a gurney.

She felt hazy. The patch must have meds in it. "Don't need drugs," she slurred, but they ignored her.

As they rolled down a narrow hallway, the lights too bright in the ceiling, the first medic said, "Glad I don't have clean-up duty."

"Didn't you know? The Norders leave the bloodstains. Stains of honor, they call them."

Annika closed her eyes and kept telling herself she wouldn't cry, but two tears squeezed out beneath her eyelids and ran down her temples. She had lost in the Blood Ring. Lost because she was soft. What would her father say?

The medics stopped in front of a white hard-sided cubicle. Every inch was occupied by tanks, monitors, metal gadgets, clips, nozzles, tubes. They extended legs out from the gurney and set it down.

One called, "Cuidada!" A small, thin woman with tired eyes appeared and bent over Annika as the medic explained what had happened. Muttering to herself, "Norders," the woman slit the patch open and peeled it off. "You're lucky, miss, that the knife didn't hit the femoral artery, or you would have bled out."

One of the medics said, "The winner twisted the knife."

"Why did she twist it?"

The medic shrugged. Annika said, her voice thick, "To make sure I didn't get up. To thrill the crowd."

"Norders." The cuidada grimaced.

She inserted plugs into Annika's nostrils. A cool mist sifted into her lungs.

Annika's stomach churned with nausea, and her eyes fluttered open. She was lying on her back. On the ceiling a forest scene slid into a sunset or a sunrise over an ocean. A lavender scent lay on the air, and below it the pungent smell of medicines. Hard white walls. Monitors and gadgets. A hospital cubicle... the Blood Ring... the crowd shouting. Liess's windpipe in her hand. Liess's longknife in her thigh. A spongy white cocoon encased her from the waist down to her toes, or where her toes should be. Embedded in the material were lights that glowed white and yellow and blue. A monitor with indecipherable lines sliding across it. Her leg. What had happened to her leg? There was no sensation from her left leg, none. She sat up and jammed her fingers under the edge of the spongy material and tried to pull it up, peel it off. Lights started blinking.

The side of the cubicle slid up, and the cuidada leaned in. "Problem?"

"My leg. What happened to my leg?"

"Healing, or it will be healing if you calm down."

Healing. Annika let out her breath and slumped back.

Peering at the monitor, the cuidada said, "I did surgery to repair muscle and tendons. There was a ligament that was nicked. What I couldn't do was clone nerves. There's not the equipment on the ship. You're in such good physical shape that instead of using artificial nerves, I kept your own. With therapy, they should heal well."

"When will I be fighting fit again? Can I go into the Blood Ring next year?"

"You took a lot of damage."

"That doesn't answer my question."

The cuidada tapped at a monitor. "It's not even two days since surgery. There's no way to tell right now."

Annika clenched the bed sheet. "I'll be back. You'll see. I'll work hard, and I'll come back to win." She would. Not this year, but next year her father would be proud of her.

As the cuidada left, she muttered, "Over two more years of Norders."

She must have put a sedative into Annika's fluids, because the next thing Annika knew, she was blinking awake, and the cuidada was holding out a holo cube. "A transmission came in from Elumet. We copied it onto a cube since there is no entertainment screen in the cubicle." She put the dark, glassy cube in Annika's hand.

"My father is in the Elumet system."

The cuidada slid her finger down the spongy cocoon, splitting it open. She looked at the leg, head tilted to one side. Annika cranked her neck around, trying to see the leg, but couldn't get a glimpse.

"And your mother?"

"Dead." Annika didn't feel like telling the story.

Mother had taken a contract as a bodyguard to a high official in the Hagen Confederation. She'd saved his life at the cost of her own. At the death service, the Council head had presented Annika with the Flying Comet award and made a speech about upholding ideals. Annika was 10 years old. She knew she should be glad her mother had performed her duty so well, but sometimes she missed her mama. Like right now. Ached with the absence. What a mommy-coddle.

The edges of the cube dug into Annika's hand. Was he going to yell at her? Tell her how disappointed he was in her? She twisted the cube, and his face came onto the screen, uniform buttoned at the throat, showing he was on duty.

"I hope you're recovering well. Remember, there's nothing you can't do if you work hard enough. So get strong and fighting fit and get back into the Blood Ring. Maybe next time I can be there to see you win." He glanced away and nodded, then turned back. "Sorry. Time to prep for an ambush." He thumped his chest with his fist and raised it. Annika murmured the phrase with him: "Courage unto death." The cube went dark.

He believed in her. She sniffed back tears.

The cuidada's voice startled her; she had forgotten the woman was in the room. "The leg is healing nicely."

"It itches."

"That's a sign you're healing."

During the following hours and days, Annika figured out how much she could do before setting off the alarms. She sweated through all the exercises she could think of. When her body felt like limp string, she studied one-on-one fighting cubes. After running through all of those once, she went through them again, interspersing them with small-group tactics. She had learned the basics, of course, in school, but there was no harm in learning more.

Two or three days later—it was hard to keep track of time—the cuidada brought in a new viewing cube. "You can read books on this. I don't know if you, uh, care for books."

"I can read." All Norders were taught to read at a rudimentary level, although they were not encouraged to read—it took time away from training and fighting and mercenary work. Her mother had insisted that she be able to understand her own contracts and had paid for tutoring in standard Galactic, even though her father said there was no need.

Shrugging, the cuidada pulled out a piece of the wall, set down the cube, and left. Annika picked up the cube, and it brightened. It was set to randomly bring up stories, poems, and essays.

Es liesse sich Alles trefflich schlichten, Könnte man die Sachen zweimal verrichten. "Everything could be beautifully adjusted if matters could be arranged a second time." Annika squeezed her eyes shut, burning with the shame of losing the fight. She could have won, should have won. If only she'd tightened her fingers.

Eventually the cocoon was removed, and two medics—maybe the same ones who had carried her out of the Blood Ring—her memory was a blur—wheeled her to her original quarters.

A marinheiro physio stopped in just as the medics were leaving. "That leg is going to need work," he said. As he checked her range of motion and strength, she was dismayed that her muscles felt like lumps of paste and her leg like a wooden club she had to drag around behind her.

He gave her some exercises and a schedule, with days off for rest and letting the body recover. But he was a marinheiro, and Norders knew they didn't push hard enough. So she always arrived early at the physio room, starting her exercises on her own before the physio was finished with other clients, and between physio sessions, she exercised in the Norder training rooms.

The first time she went into a training room was hard. Very hard. Conversation stopped when she limped in. Her cheeks burned. But then someone said, "Bad luck. You almost had her," and someone else said,

"Better luck next time." Occasionally she saw someone from her year-group and would stop to talk—catch up on who had gotten a new contract, who had died. She heard that Liess, now a two-time Blood Ring champion, had an apartment with the clan leaders and took meals with them.

One day, as Annika was leaving the training room, she ran into Liess. Her heart seemed to drop out of her chest.

"Good fight," Liess said.

Annika mouthed what was expected. "You were better. But wait until next year."

Liess fingered the jeweled brooch on her vest. "Let's have a practice match sometime. As soon as you're better, that is." As Liess walked away, Annika noticed the man she was with—a tall, thin, black-haired marinheiro. Odd. Norders and marinheiros tended not to mix.

Over time, Annika's muscles hardened, and her leg improved, but it was a little stiff and slow and tired easily. No one would call her fighting fit. She knew she needed to spend more time working out and less time sleeping.

After a few weeks, the physio did a scan of the leg and hip, re-tested her range of motion and strength, and announced that he had done all he could. "You worked harder than anyone else," he assured her, but there was a lot of scar tissue. The leg wouldn't get better. There were other patients on his roster. He apologized again.

With an impassive face, Annika nodded. "I see... Yes. Right."

When she got back to her apartment, the screen notified her that she had been moved from the injured list to the disabled category.

Numbly, she lay down on the bedshelf and stared at the bare, blank ceiling. She couldn't move. Tried not to think. She was frozen, inside and out.

The console pinged with a message from her father. He had heard about her assignment to the disabled category. "Couldn't that greasy-fingered marinheiro surgeon fix you up? Maybe once you are in the new home you can get some decent surgery. In the meantime, work hard on your rehab. I know you will be fighting fit in no time."

He didn't understand. She could not have worked harder. And the cuidada had done the best she could. Maybe more surgery would help. Maybe not. Even if surgery brought her back physically, she might not be able to hone herself mentally to a peak fighting edge. She thought she might cry, but tears did not come. Her body was dry and empty.

A few hours later she saw by the clock that it was night. Few people would be moving around the ship. Good. She wouldn't have to talk to anyone. She got up and headed out—she didn't know where. Just out. The corridor lamps were dimmed, and it was quiet.

Odors of sweat and citrus air cleaner and powder reached her nose. Her feet had taken her to one of the training rooms. Even at this time of night, a handful of Norders were working out, but Annika found a free resistance machine. After a few minutes a stocky man stepped off the treadmill and towelled the sweat off his face. Annika had often seen him in the training rooms. He approached her. "I'm on a training regimen for the Gold Ring and have to use this machine next." He was half-apologetic. "Maybe you can run for a while." It was understood that those in training or undergoing therapy had priority. How many times had Annika displaced others without thinking about it twice? But now she was being bumped.

Trying not to let the surge of shame show on her face, she stopped and released her grip. "I was done anyway," she lied. As she limped out of the training room, the resistance machine quickened its thump-thump-thump as the man settled into his exercise.

The next night she walked through corridors at random, avoiding people when she saw them. In a back corridor a Norder stooped to roll up worn and dirty floor matting. His hair was white, and his knuckles were big with arthritis. Norders who were not in training or on a contract contributed labor to the community and to the running of the ship. As a Ring fighter, Annika had always been exempt. Now she felt like the matting—worn and battered. She should be taken to the recycling tanks and turned into something useful.

As the days passed, she fell into a routine of lying in her room all day and ghosting down corridors at night. If she was hungry and happened to be passing a pantry, she grabbed a little bread and cheese. Mostly, though, the thought of eating made her throat feel dry and thick, like she couldn't swallow. Her clothing draped loosely on her.

One evening Liess and her marinheiro friend turned into her corridor and were walking toward her, but they were talking so intently that Annika was able to back away without being spotted.

Then there was the Wild. It soothed Annika as nothing else did. Just sitting by the pond, hearing an occasional quack of a duck or the plop of a frog, walking the trails, exploring off-trail. Sometimes she wished she could get lost, but the Wild was not big enough. There were no mountains, but Annika could climb a grassy hill and look out. When you stood in the forest you could see the Big Lake curving up until it looked like the water would fall out. But when she was at the lake, the trees climbed up the sides. Far above, a lamp moved on a track down the "sky" and brightened and dimmed to make days and nights, synchronized with the rest of the ship. The "sun" would move one way, and the "moon" would follow the path back.

One morning when she returned to her apartment after a night of roaming, the console blinked with a message. She had never replied to her father's message, hadn't known what to say. Was he following up? No. It was from the marinheiro ship purser, telling her to report to Sector 1, Level 1, Blue 14 for a temporary assignment. Was she already reduced to rolling up dirty matting? Her stomach turned over.

After all of her wanderings, she knew where Sector 1, Level 1 was: near the main ports and airlocks.

She found the right area but had to wait because marinheiros were clustering by the main airlock. From scraps of conversation she gathered they would be docking soon at a small waystation, where some of the crew were scheduled to do a little trading.

When she finally checked in with a clerk, the marinheiro gave her a once-over, muttered, "About a medium-tall," and then handed her a plain gray suit that looked metallic but was flexible. A heavy odor clung to its interior, like old sweat and farts and chemical cleaners.

Annika pointed to other suits, each on its own stand, crowding the space behind the clerk. They looked newer, bright and clean, in a medley of colors and decorations. Some had thumb-sized boosters hanging from the collar so the wearer could control the suit with electrical impulses from the brain. "How about one of those?"

"Those suits, they belong to us, the marinheiros. Everyone has their own suit made to specifications. You get a standard work suit."

He continued, "You can put your shoes over there, on the shelves." Ignoring the wrinkling of Annika's nose, the marinheiro helped stuff her legs and arms into the suit and shove boots on her feet. "Watch how you walk; they're magnetized to stick to the hull so you don't go flying off."

A smelly suit? Mag boots? The equipment was really old. "I trained in mag boots. About a thousand years ago."

"You want the longknife outside the suit?"

She stared at him. "What use is it if it's inside?"

"I suppose you Norders want your knives handy in case of a bear attack."

Annika barked a laugh. "*Allzeit bereit!* That's what we say. Always be prepared."

"You a righty or a lefty?"

"Righty."

He cinched a belt around the outside of the suit and started to arrange the sheath on her right side. She said, "I have to draw the knife with my right hand." The clerk and Annika stared at each other, the clerk baffled and Annika irritated.

"It goes on my left side, where I can draw it." Not quite below his hearing, she muttered, "Idiot."

He shrugged, moved the sheath to her left hip, clipped a heater to the belt, and handed her a bubble-shaped helmet. Wires so tiny she almost couldn't see them sparkled in the helmet's clear plastic.

"Don't put the helmet on until you're ready to go out. No need to waste the oxygen pack."

"What will I be doing?"

"Scrubbing barnacles. Go to the airlock down the hall and wait with the rest of the workers."

Scrubbing barnacles. She really was old and worn.

She turned in the direction he pointed. With every step the suit flexed, and a new puff of odor hit her nose. She shifted the helmet from under one arm to the other.

Suddenly, striding down the corridor toward her were Liess and her marinheiro beanpole. Annika lowered her head and tried to reach the airlock before Liess noticed her.

"Good day, Annika." Yellow jewels dangled at Liess's ears and decorated her tunic. "You haven't been to the training rooms lately."

"Not lately." Annika tried to scuttle around her.

Liess looked at her suit, her eyes moving down to the helmet under Annika's arm and the heater on her belt. "Looks like you're going barnacle-scrubbing," she teased.

Annika blushed hotly.

Liess smirked. "You *are* going barnacle-scrubbing." She motioned for the marinheiro to follow as she walked away, shoulders heaving as she tried to suppress her laughter.

Annika still felt flushed as she arrived at the airlock.

Five marinheiros in colorful suits were standing next to the airlock's console. Four Norders sat on nearby benches, an older man and three youngsters, maybe 10 or 12 years old. They were chatting as they waited. Annika sat on a bench away from them, placing the helmet next to her as a barrier.

"The Blood Ring takes a quick knife." A boy was talking to the elder, whose cheek was puckered with scar tissue. The elder ran a hand over his massive head, rasping the bristles of his gray hair. "It's strength that counts in the Blood Ring, muscle and meat."

The boy boasted, "I'm going to be Blood Ring Champion one day."

The elder darted a glance at Annika, who kept her head down. She was sure he recognized her. She caught herself massaging her injured thigh and jerked her hand away.

The two girls were comparing their new shortknives, showing the metalwork and enamel inlay of the hilts. This was what Annika had been reduced to. Scrubbing barnacles with elders and children.

A marinheira with a tray of coffee cups stopped. First, she offered the cups to the Norders. "Coffee?" They declined. Most Norders didn't like the sludgy, sweet brew. The marinheiros reached for the heavy white cups in a tangle of arms.

In the distance metal crashed against metal, and there was a jolt.

The marinheira lurched, cups rattling. One of the marinheiros, a man with brown hair pulled back in a tail, put a hand around her waist. "Steady there."

She tossed her head. "Watch the hands."

A marinheiro in an iridescent green suit—he hardly looked past boyhood—said, "The pilot made a rough docking, right, João?"

João was a middle-aged marinheiro with plump cheeks and streaks of gray in his hair. "The waystation tractors, they were clumsy. It's not so hard to bring in a cylinder like this one. Easy as butter. Not like a hub-and-spoke, where everything has to line up."

A green light appeared on the instrument panel set into the wall, and a pleasant voice said, "Everything is green to go. Repeat. Green to go."

The crew took last sips of coffee and put the cups back down on the tray. The man with the tail of hair said to the woman, "How about a kiss for luck?"

She tossed her head. "You think all the women are waiting to kiss Madio." But she swung her hips and glanced back over her shoulder as she walked away.

One of the marinheiro men stood and faced the Norders. "I am Third Mate Felipe da Silva V, leading the work group." He looked young to be a Third Mate, maybe in his thirties, dark hair clipped close to his head. "While we are docked at the waystation we'll refuel and do a systems check and maintenance. First Mate wants to take the opportunity to give the ship a good cleaning for barnacle spores. They float through space and attach to ships. If they aren't burned off, eventually they'll burrow all the way through the hull and cause air leakages.

"Some of you Norders have never been barnacle-scrubbing. Just follow instructions from the crew members."

A woman in a suit with orange swirls approached Annika. Most of her hair was buzzed short, but a lock over the left ear was long and braided with shells and feathers. She smiled hesitantly. "Hello. You're Miss Annika, right? I'm Tereza da Silva."

"All right," Annika mumbled.

The marinheira's smile became a little fixed. "Nice to meet you. A pleasure." She reached for the heater at Annika's belt and tilted it up. "Medium heat. Perfect. The spores look like white pillows nestling into the hull. Heat them long enough so they shrivel up."

A light on the panel flashed red. The smooth, calm contralto said, "Attention. Atmosphere venting in Sector H. Repeat. Atmosphere is venting in Sector H."

The third mate's eyes widened. He reached for the console's communicator, shot a glance at the Norders, and muted it. His lips moved.

Annika found herself on her feet, along with the elder Norder, their bodies automatically taking the "ready" stance, weight over the balls of the feet, longknives in their hands, arms a little away from their sides, eyes scanning left, right, up, down.

A dull boom. That was a wave gun. Her heart thudded faster.

Third Mate lifted his helmet. "We've been boarded. Pirates from the waystation."

The elder started down the corridor at a trot, away from the airlock and back toward the check-in area where they'd been outfitted with their suits and heaters. Toward the wave gun. Hands went to knives, and the other Norders jostled after him. Annika tried to follow, but her bad leg had stiffened and made her stumble. She was grabbed from behind and shaken. Third Mate said, "Keep your brains together. You're going to fight a wave gun with a heater and a knife?"

Boom. Boom. Someone gasped, "Getting closer."

The pleasant contralto said, "Losing air pressure, Sector B. Repeat. Losing air pressure, Sector B." Silence for a moment. Then, "To the lifeboats and shelters. Seek out lifeboats and shelters. Repeat. Seek out lifeboats and shelters."

Orange suit—Tereza—paused with her head to one side. "The wave gun is between us and the B sector's lifeboat. And the shelter is way the other side."

So. They needed to come up with some kind of safe place and get moving. The marinheiros stood rigid, heads jerking back and forth, not knowing what to do. Corpsicles, her field instructor would have called them, frozen in bewilderment, soon to be dead. Annika's thoughts were coming quick and clear. She pushed her face up to Third Mate's, to get his attention. "We'll be cornered here. We need to go out onto the hull and then in through another airlock. Like bunnies. Bunnies don't have big teeth, but they have a back door."

Boom. Boom. Boom. The wave gun was getting closer, its frequencies buzzing in her feet.

"But where? They're taking control and venting atmosphere sector by sector."

"The Wild. Lots of air."

A brief pause. "Right." Now that there was a plan, he acted. "Madio. Lock the hatch to the rest of the ship. Tereza, Agostino, all the O-packs you can grab in the next two minutes. João, cycle the airlock. Everyone, helmets on, radios off." He slammed his own helmet shut.

Annika got her helmet halfway on, but it got stuck. She swore, lifted it off, got it seated tight. Everyone swarmed into the airlock. Air hissed. The outer hatch opened.

Annika turned on the magnetic boots before walking onto the hull. Her brain couldn't decide if she was standing up or falling into a black, starry sky. Her stomach flipped back and forth.

Above or below her head was an expanse of black dotted with sharp points of light. Her boots were pressed against the gray hull of the ship. The hull curved in front of her, the horizon line sharp. Impossible to tell how far away it was. Her sense of scale was utterly confused. In the absence of an atmosphere, there was no blurring and blue-shifting of distant objects. Familiar objects for comparison were lacking. The hull's protuberances and fins could be small and close or large and far away. Light from her right put sharp-edged shadows on the hull in faithful silhouettes of the six people in the group. She realized it must be light from the waystation.

Was she falling head first? Her stomach flipped again. Boots are down, head is up, Annika chanted to herself. Boots down, head up.

Third Mate started down the hull in a skating motion followed by the other crew members. They were all wearing socklike boots, probably with nanobots to grip the metal. The mag boots clung to the metal hull with each step, and she had to lift the foot off. Step-pull, step-pull. It didn't take a lot of effort, but it was annoying.

She drew her longknife and heater and took on the job of rear guard, her body tight with tension, remaining alert and scanning the whole area, frequently checking behind them. She'd go down fighting.

Step-pull, step-pull. Her thigh muscles were beginning to cramp. Since the Blood Ring her hair had gotten shaggy, and now it clung warm and damp to her neck and forehead, except for one piece that kept getting in her left eye. Her fingers kept reaching up to brush it away and kept bumping into her visor. Now she knew why the marinheiros cropped their hair short or wore it long enough to tie back.

The marinheiros had dwindled and disappeared behind the curve of the ship's hull. Annika kept going. Damn—she wasn't lost, was she? The marinheiros would surely realize she was missing. Did this ancient suit have a light? Fumbling, she found a switch, and a spot of harsh white light appeared on the hull.

Now the orange suit appeared and grew bigger and bigger. It stopped and touched her helmet to Annika's. The voice resonated through the glass and air to Annika's ears. "We're heading starboard toward sector C."

"Okay."

Annika followed her, and in a few minutes, they caught up to the rest of the group who were sitting in the sharp-edged shadow of a tall fin. Someone in a striped suit was swapping out an O-pack. Annika leaned against the fin, afraid that if she sat down her leg wouldn't be able to push her up again. The fin was surprisingly warm, maybe to bleed off excess heat from the ship.

Tereza appeared to be sipping at her drinking tube. Some of the marinheiros were chewing. Of course, Annika's suit provided no water or food. Okay. In field training she had learned to hike and work on scant supplies.

Something sparkled up like a fountain above the hull. Pretty. She touched Third Mate's shoulder and tilted her head toward it. He stood and looked, then put his helmet against Annika's. "They're venting more air. That must be C sector."

A small boat the size of a shuttlecraft drifted away from the ship. The marinheiros touched each other's arms and pointed. It seemed to hang in space for long moments, then jets flared, and it leaped away. The marinheiros threw their arms in the air; some embraced each other.

Annika stared after the lifeboat, so small and alone, willing it to keep going. It dwindled to an iridescent beetle, a spark, and then it was gone.

What was happening to Liess and her marinheiro friend? To the elder Norder who had tried to attack the wave gun, what about the children who had followed him? Dead, probably. She blinked, hard. Grief could come later. She would burn paper for them, release their memories into ash and smoke.

Third Mate put his helmet against Annika's. "Are you ready to move on?"

"Yes."

The marinheiros glided away. Annika step-pulled after them.

Third Mate stopped, and his hands reached out in graceful gestures as if sculpting air. The other marinheiros lifted hands and nodded. The older man, João, leaned over a console recessed in an airlock. He pressed something, looked at a monitor, then moved over to a portal. The two men conferred. Annika pressed her helmet against theirs. She caught mentions of "float tubes" and "but if the power is cut" and "smashed dead".

Third Mate said, "We'll have to go inside the ship and take the corridors."

João reached for the airlock handle. Annika said, "If the pirates have taken over the entire ship, they might be on the other side of the airlock. Wave guns, needlers. Don't cycle the airlock, in case it alerts them. Just open the door manually and rush in."

Third Mate nodded. His smile glinted. "Like bunnies."

Annika nodded. "I'll go first." She drew her longknife and heater. The only marinheiro with his heater out was Third Mate. She rolled her eyes. She had to remember that the marinheiros were not Norders. "Tell them to draw their heaters. And turn them on high." He nodded, and his hands sculpted the air again.

Annika drew a few deep breaths, shook out her legs as best she could, and nodded to João. The outer door opened. The inner door opened, and she charged in.

No wave guns. No people. All quiet. Her muscles relaxed, and she sighed in relief. The marinheiros came after her. Someone bumped her in the back. They really were not Norders. João closed the doors.

It looked like a service area, with an infinity of struts and pillars and panels with twinkling lights. One of the pillars had a bundle of wires dangling from an open panel. A food wrapper stirred in a wisp of air. Since it hadn't been blown out the airlock, Annika figured most of this sector's atmosphere had already been vented.

João examined the console and spoke with Third Mate, who then walked over to Annika. "This sector shows no activity. We're going to take a rest break." She nodded. Her bad leg was tired and aching. The marinheiros were stooped and stumbling with fatigue.

After a few minutes Third Mate got them up and moving again. Eventually they came to a vertical ladder leading up to a circular hatch. Felipe told Annika. "The Wild."

"I'll reconnoiter. Everyone else, stay here." Her bad leg cramped and twinged as she climbed the ladder, but she tried not to show it. Quietly she unclipped the hatch and raised it just enough to peer around. Grasses and twigs stirred as air rushed into the service area. Fortunately, the hatch was in the middle of a stand of close-growing trees, giving her cover. She climbed out and closed the hatch. It clanged. She removed her helmet and left it by the hatch. On her belly, she crawled to the edge of the trees to look out.

She was at the edge of the silverbark woods. In front of her was a meadow and beyond it Big Lake, sprinkled with ducks.

In the meadow a miniature deer, no taller than her knees, stood motionless, ears lifted, as three people emerged from farther down in the woods. They wore battlesuits with thickened breastplates, leg guards, and helmets that looked like turtle shells, the visors raised. Two carried heavy blasters. The shoulders of the third were bowed under the weight of a disassembled wave gun, the barrel running lengthwise down his back, power pack and synchronizer strapped on top. The deer leaped away. Annika clenched the right side of her jaw to turn up the hearing augment.

The one in the lead said in standard Galactic with a twittery accent, "That's what you heard, a deer."

"It sounded more metallic," another insisted with a raspy voice.

The one bent under the wave gun laughed. "Probably not a Norder. They're battle-mad. Boss had good strategy—they ran right at our weapons."

The first one twittered, "Carky said the marinheiros tried to seal off the control room, but he and his troops used the codes to get in. Pilot plugged in real easy. Once she gestalted with the computer, we ruled the ship."

Raspy voice again. "You have to win the ground too. There are probably some crew and Norders left in the nooks and crannies, but the only sector with significant atmosphere is this one, and we cleaned it out. Now we can seal ourselves snug in the control room, and there's not much anyone can do to us."

Twittery said, "It's a pretty place. A shame if Boss closes it down."

"She said not to vent; when the buyer gets here they'll decide what to do."

The three reached the main entrance. They closed their visors and cycled through the lock.

Annika waited a few minutes to make sure they were not coming back, then undid the hatch and motioned to the marinheiros. As they clambered up, one by one, she ran her fingers through sweat-damp hair and gulped in scents of sweet grass and clover. Insects buzzed a dry tune. Safe. For now. No one knew better than she did how quickly things could change.

After the whole group had climbed up and stood panting, Annika reported what she had seen and heard.

Third Mate's hands closed into fists. "So. The pirates have the ship."

João said, "One lifeboat, at least, got away. And we have shelters in each sector." He crossed himself. "I pray that many are safe."

Anger began to burn in Annika's chest. "Lifeboats and shelters for marinheiros. Where are the seats for the Norders? Is there room in the hiding holes for the Norders?"

Someone sucked in a breath. Another started to speak but stopped.

Third Mate wheeled to face her, raising his chin. " If there is only one seat left in the lifeboat, the marinheiro gives it to the client. If there is no space in the shelter, a marinheiro leaves so the client can enter. If there is only one oxygen pack, it is the client who breathes."

Silence. Now Annika remembered the orientation guide saying something about emergencies—just before she had ducked out. She said, "I didn't know. I'm sorry." She thought of her mother, who had died for the man she had been guarding. She forced herself to give a formal apology, looking at each marinheiro in turn. "Now I understand. My words shame me."

João said, "We are all one, now. We must hold together."

Felipe extended his arm, and Annika grasped it briefly above the elbow, feeling solid muscle under the suit's fabric. She said, "And now I am going to glue my lips together."

He said, "The ranger cabin will have food, drinks, blankets."

The marinheiros moved away quickly. Annika retrieved her helmet and slipped off her mag boots, wanting to hurl them into the woods. She clipped them to her belt instead. The grass and dry dirt felt good under her toes.

When they got to the ranger cabin, Felipe instructed them not to touch any of the electronics. "The toilets have electronic chips too. Use nothing that was made later than the Stone Age."

Tereza hesitated, her hand on the door latch. "What if someone is inside—dead?"

Annika snorted. "It's the live bodies you have to worry about. I'll scout." Then she stopped. Her field instructor used to say, "There can be only one number one." Third Mate outranked everyone else here, and she was gaining respect for his calmness and intelligence and decision-making. She looked at him. "What do you think?" she asked him, and he nodded to go ahead.

She drew her longknife and heater.

The door swung open easily. A hologram display of animals and plants occupied the central part of the room. Information monitors flickered, eerily quiet. Toilets to the left. Thoroughness had been her field instructor's watchword. Annika checked each pod.

Down a hallway were several doors. One opened to a room with bunkbeds piled with blankets, four altogether. Next, a small office. A kitchen with a bin of canned and dried foods, a cooker, and a cooler, still running.

Out the back door was a lean-to shed, and here Annika struck gold. Packs of food cubes, squeeze bulbs of water and coffee—Annika was thirsty, but it would have to be ignored until she finished scouting—tools, oxygen packs, a medkit, a couple of spacesuits, two tranquilizer guns, several tanglecords, and three heaters. Blasters and nerve disruptors would be better, but she would take heaters. And in the clearing behind the cabin, a firepit. Seeing bootprints, she deduced the three pirates had been there and left without looting. She went into the trees behind the cabin. Nothing out of the ordinary.

She went around to the front to let the marinheiros know all was well. For the moment, anyway.

Everyone shucked off their suits. Odor from her suit clung to Annika's skin and clothing. "I'm going to the pond. Bath time."

At the pond's edge she peeled off her sweaty clothing and examined her body. So thin. It needed more meat and muscle. Thin scar lines were souvenirs of knife fights. A shiny disc on her ribs was from a heater when she had been too slow and clumsy in the Silver Ring. Liess's knife had left lumpy scar tissue on her left thigh.

Her father's skin bore scars upon scars. When Annika was training, sometimes her father would point at his scars and talk about how he had earned them. Even though Annika had heard the stories many times, she always liked hearing them again. "What about that one, Father?"

That night, Felipe approved a tiny fire. "It seems clear that the pirates have all consolidated in the ship's control area and are not patrolling. They'll be watching the monitors. A fire shouldn't show up, not like using electrical heating units. And there's something comforting about wood smoke." They all sat around the firepit. She had considered setting a lookout, but she'd hear the main lock if it opened or if the atmosphere started to vent. They were all shocked and fatigued in body and spirit and needed rest, warmth, food, and companionship.

No one had the heart to prepare a meal, so they chewed on food cubes. Tereza sat hugging her knees to her chest, sleeves from a ranger jacket dangling below her hands. "Shouldn't we be rationing the food?"

The last of her cube wadded up in Annika's mouth, and she had to swallow hard to get the salty mass down. It reminded her of field training and sitting around fires like this one, everyone telling stories. At the time Annika would have snorted with laughter if anyone had told her she'd be nostalgic about food cubes.

When her throat was clear she waved an arm from under the blanket draped over her shoulders. "Fresh food all around. Green stuff. Meat on the hoof."

"You mean eat live animals?"

"Of course we would cook them first. What do you think goes into the kitchen pots?"

Felipe put in, "A lot of marinheiros don't eat meat. We serve it to Norders, of course. It's in our contract."

Madio muttered, "There's a lot in our contract."

From the woods came a voice and a scuffling noise. Annika leaped up, longknife in her hand, hearing augment clicked on, nostrils flared to catch scent. Into the firelight stumbled a slim marinheira in damp, muddy clothing, red hair clumped with mud. Her mouth quivered. "I'm so glad to see you."

"Isabel!" Tereza leaped up to embrace the woman. The others took turns greeting her and patting her on the back.

Felipe asked, "Is anyone else out there?"

Isabel shook her head as she sank to the ground. "I don't think so." She swiped at tears, smearing mud on her cheeks. "I was so scared."

"What happened?" Tereza put her arm around Isabel's shoulders.

"I was at the marsh lab. Everyone else had left, going to visit the waystation, but I wanted to check on the cattails. I was enjoying the quiet. Then I heard a biosensor humming and a wave gun firing. It was so stupid—I wasn't thinking—I went to see what was going on, and I saw three people in suits. They didn't see me. I ran to the marsh and found a

130

big stand of cattails and ducked into them. I went almost all the way under water. They went right by me. I could hear them crashing around. I stayed in a long time, because I was afraid they'd pick me up on the biosensor. It got so cold. Then I was just wandering around in the dark, until I saw your fire." She was shivering so hard her teeth chattered.

Tereza handed her a squeeze bulb of hot coffee. João went inside and brought out a blanket, wrapping it around her as if she were a child, tucking the ends under her chin.

"Obrigada, João."

The young man—Agostino—said, "I would have fought them." His voice cracked on the word "fought."

João said, "Then you would be dead and cold, not sitting by the fire with us. And what good would that do anyone?"

Annika asked, "What will the pirates do now?"

Isabel jumped a little and peered across the fire. "Norder?"

Tereza explained, "Miss Annika was with our work crew when the ship was boarded. Oh, this is my cousin, Isabellina da Silva." Tereza went on, "The shuttle that pulled away while we were eating must have taken some of the pirates away, maybe back to home base." Annika hadn't noticed, but the crew must be as aware of the ship as she was of her own body. Tereza's fingers reached up to tug at her lock of hair. "They're probably down to a small crew in the control room, waiting for the buyer."

Annika was surprised. "A few crew? For this big ship?"

Felipe nodded. "It doesn't take a lot of people to keep the ship running for a short time. So much is automated."

He poked the fire with a stick, sending up sparks. "But what I want to know is how they got into the control room. How did they get their pilot into gestalt to operate the ship. There is security. There are codes, retina scans."

Madio said, "Shouldn't we look for other survivors?" Annika remembered him flirting with the coffee girl.

After a time, Felipe answered. "No. Each group is on its own. If we use radio the pirates can track us down. And if we did locate another group, what would we do? How could we save them?" He fell silent.

Annika heard the words he had not spoken. How can we even save ourselves?

One night her field instructor had scooped up some pebbles and closed her lean fingers around them. "What happens if a stone is added?" Annika and the other trainees had shaken their heads, not sure what the instructor was getting at. She nodded at Annika. "Put another stone in my fist." Annika picked up a stone and pushed it in between the thumb and forefinger, but a stone dropped out the other side. "Your mind is like my fist," the instructor said. "It can hold only a few thoughts at a time."

What the marinheiros needed was something to think about besides pirates. Annika shoved herself to her feet. "Time for me to get my beauty sleep. Tomorrow we'll plan how to take back the ship." She winked at Felipe. Faces jerked toward her. Mouths dropped open. Agostino muttered, "She's missing a couple of jets."

But everyone seemed to think it was a good idea to rest. Most of them went into the cabin to sleep. Madio went in but brought out blankets and laid them on the ground beside the fire.

Annika's left leg ached and had stiffened into a block of wood. She shook it out and stamped the ground until she could walk on it. Tereza whispered to Felipe, "She's handicapped. She should have a bunk."

"She is tough as a piece of boot leather and could sleep in a bramble bush, but she shall have a bunk because she is Norder and a client."

Boot leather, was she? Annika liked that. "I'm going to have a cozy bed by the fire under what passes for the moon." She shook out her blanket and folded it on the ground, making a bedroll.

In the middle of a pleasant dream—something about field training in a pine forest—she woke up. Twigs cracked.

Hand to knife. Quiet. Still. Listening. Easing open an eyelid. A pile of blankets where Madio had been. The cracking was moving away, but not in the direction of the latrine.

She got up and crept after Madio. When she said his name, he whirled around, raising his heater and dropping the spacesuit he had bundled under his arm.

"You going to go off to be a hero, rescue the coffee girl?"

"How do you—? What do you care?"

"We're going to take back the ship. The whole ship. Rescue everybody. But we are just a few, and we need you."

He flung up his hands. "But…"

"You don't know where to find her, or even if she's still…" Annika was going to say "alive," but substituted "on the ship."

"I have to try." Now he didn't look much older than Agostino.

The longknife was still in her hand. She pushed it back into the sheath at her hip. "Look. I have experience." Some days of classroom learning, a few months of field training, some holos as her leg had healed. "We can take back the ship. If she's in a shelter, we can rescue her safe and whole. But running blindly around the ship is going to put us all at risk."

He sagged. "You're right. I just want to do something."

"Tomorrow." She led him back toward the fire. "Let me show you how to walk soft-footed in the woods."

After that, Annika slept deep and sweet until the clicking of a firestarter woke her. Isabel was on her knees by the firepit trying to light a pile of wood. Next to her on the ground sat a coffee percolator. She must have been to the pond to bathe, because her hair and skin were damp and clean. Annika stretched. The artificial sunlight felt good on her face. "There's squeeze bulbs of coffee in the lean-to," Annika offered.

"Nothing like fresh-brewed."

Annika couldn't stand to watch any longer. "Here. You have to arrange the wood, not just pile it up. And you need some tinder." Soon Annika had a fire going, and the percolator was giving off a delicious fragrance. The others stumbled out of the cabin looking disheveled and tired.

Isabel poured thick dark coffee and spooned in sugar. She offered the first cup to Annika, who took it and sipped to be polite. She felt not like a stranger, exactly, but like a guest. After working with the marinheiros to evade pounding by a wave gun, to clamber over the hull, and sneak through the ship, it was uncomfortable.

For breakfast they chewed on food cubes. No one mentioned hunting game.

Felipe nibbled at his food cube, then set it aside. "So. The pirates likely have just a few crew members on board, and all in the control room."

João put in, "Pirates with burners and wave guns."

Tereza mumbled around a mouthful of food cube, "There wouldn't be a reason for them to set up a wave gun in the control room or have crew standing around with burners in their hands."

"Still, it's burners against heaters."

Annika put in, "We'll be wearing spacesuits. And the pirates will be feeling safe. They think they got rid of any fightback."

Felipe picked up a stick and began to draw lines in the dirt. "This is the control room. I have the security codes in my head, and the ship will accept my retina scan."

Isabel had begun to gather up cups and cube wrappers, but she set them down with a clatter. "Wait. Wait. Why don't we just surrender? Wouldn't they put us on a lifeboat and send us away?"

Annika said, "Why bother? Why not just burn us down or shove us out the nearest airlock? Much simpler."

Agostino gulped.

Isabel's eyebrows drew together. "You don't know that. There's a chance. There's no chance of us going up against them and winning."

Madio said, "What about all the other people sheltering on the ship? We might get away, but they would be stuck."

"But…"

Felipe's face set into stern lines. His eyes could cut steel. "It is our ship. And we are going to take it back." He continued drawing. "They're probably using the captain's quarters for sleeping and eating. It connects with the control room, here, on the side."

Annika eyed the sketch. "Is there a door in between or is it just open?"

"Of course there's a door."

"Does it lock?"

"Of course it doesn't lock." He was eyeing her as if she were an idiot, then seemed to remember that she wouldn't know. "The door is for privacy, but crew would never enter without permission."

The stick dug into the other side of captain's quarters. "There is another door into the main hallway." He smiled slightly at her. "The back door, for bunnies. That does lock."

Annika thought. "Half of us could go in through the control room and half through that back door."

"I don't have the codes. That is private, the captain's personal entrance."

"How about if we confuse them by making them think they're being attacked at the captain's private door? Rig something up to make noise? Or emit smoke?" She brightened. "Poison gas?"

"Combustion requires oxygen. That corridor has likely been vented. Maybe we could use carbon monoxide. João?"

João ran fingers through his thick gray hair. "I'd have to research it. On the other hand, a knocker would be easy. Something to go off on a timer and bang on the door. I'll look through the cabin's equipment with Agostino. He's clever with tools and machinery."

It was hard to imagine Agostino being clever with anything, but she trusted João. "Good. Great. While the machine is knocking on the back door, we'll be visiting through the front door. Confuse the hell out of them."

"What do you want us to do now?" Felipe asked, putting down his stick.

"Drill." Annika gave a sharp nod. "We have to move quickly, before the buyer arrives."

All afternoon she had them work against each other with the heaters off. They needed to get used to handling the heaters and pointing them at people. "Blister their faces, they'll drop their guns. When they use their hands to cover their faces, blister their hands. Heat their clothing, make it catch on fire. Don't worry about a wave gun. If you keep them busy, they won't get a chance to set it up."

Isabel held her heater as far away from her body as her arms would reach, and she kept dropping it. The fourth time she picked it up off the ground, glaring at Annika as if it were her fault, Annika sighed. Her field instructor had said, "If you can't fit the person to the job, fit the job to the person." She went to the lean-to and returned with the tanglecords. "You're going to like this part. You're going to tie me up." Annika handed her a cord. "These are tanglecords. They're also called python cords. Put a loop around a head or arm or neck, and press here—it'll wrap itself around the person and tighten."

Isabel dithered and dropped the cord but finally got one around Annika's arm. It snaked around Annika's torso, up the other arm, around the legs, and snugged tight. It was uncomfortable, good, that was the right way to do it. Annika said, "Now press that green button to loosen." Isabel pressed it, and the cord relaxed. Shucking it off, Annika said, "Good job. You're in charge of tying up pirates."

To the group, she said, "Don't worry about your buddies. Focus on your own targets. You can help your friends when you are in total control of your own zone."

She told an old anecdote about a soldier who tried to help his buddy and got the whole squad killed. She didn't know if it was true, but there was nothing like a good story to drive a point home.

"I'll lead the charge, get a visual of the situation. Then I'll fall back to support the team and give orders." She glanced at Felipe for his approval.

"Sounds like a good plan."

Annika chuckled. "It'll be a plan for about a minute. Then it'll be a madhouse. You know what they say, 'No plan survives first contact with the enemy.' " Blank looks on their faces. They'd find out.

That night by the fire they sat quietly. Tereza and Isabel had their heads close together and were talking in low tones. João and Agostino were working on the knocker, an ungainly looking contraption of metal and wood with a power pack, all sitting on a wheeled wooden base. João was shining a hand light over the contraption and talking about gear ratios. Agostino adjusted the power pack with a thin tool. Felipe and Madio seemed deep in their own thoughts.

Annika had found a knife used for cutting meat and was hacking off her hair. Damn if she was going to have it falling in her face during battle.

Felipe came over to sit next to her. "We—the crew—know how to run the ship—but not how to defend her. We were unprepared for the attack. Woefully unprepared."

"Got caught with your britches down." She hacked off a chunk of hair, watched it float to the ground, gleaming in the firelight. "We Norders

136

did not help save the ship or passengers or crew. The pirate was right. We just charged into battle, our only concern to show our bravery."

"You helped. You are helping now. And," he took a breath. "I hope you will help in the future. I want to hire you to train us, when this is over." He paused and gave a wintry smile. "Assuming I'm alive, of course."

Annika's hand stopped halfway through a wad of hair. It wasn't mercenary work. It wasn't bodyguard work. In short, it wasn't Norder work. But if they actually pulled it off, if they recaptured the ship—the marinheiros were good people, hard workers, smart. But they needed her. She'd be good at this. But what would her father think? He was very far away. Annika would deal with that when she had to. She cut another hunk of hair. "I'd like that. Assuming I'm alive, of course."

The next day they gathered next to the hatch in the woods where they had entered. They were suited up, helmets off, extra O-packs on their backs, and heaters clipped to their belts. Isabel carried a heater and the tanglecords. They'd decided to approach the control room through the empty ship rather than go out onto the hull.

Felipe said, "Miss Annika, do you have any words for us?"

This was the first time she had been asked for a battle speech. She hesitated. "I'm proud of you. You trained hard." She added, "You're all nice people, but you can't be nice in battle. The pirates killed your families, massacred your friends." She thumped her fist to her chest. "Courage unto death." They echoed her. "Courage unto death."

Felipe cautioned them as he opened the hatch. "Nothing to set off an alarm. Ladders, not lifters. Hallways, not sliders. We will be little bunnies in the walls."

Annika grinned as she got ready to put on her helmet. "Rats. Big rats with sharp teeth."

Felipe took the lead, and Annika took the rear. They made their way through airless service areas lit by strips of emergency lighting, through hatches that already stood open.

They came to a residential sector. The fiber matting was rucked up, and textile hangings were tattered with burned edges. The marinheiros had gotten ahead of Annika and were clustered around something on the floor. Annika pushed herself to catch up.

Bodies sprawled randomly, marinheiros and Norders, flesh puckered and rippled by wave gun fire. With the tips of her suit fingers, Isabel brushed a lock of shining black hair away from a face. Her mouth contorted; her face reddened. She ducked her head and pounded on her helmet with both hands. Tereza laid a hand on Isabel's arm. João made the sign of the cross on his chest.

Annika didn't know anyone in the sad group, but she thrust her arm into the air to get the marinheiros' attention, curled her fingers into a fist, and thumped her chest. They nodded and sped down the corridor.

Soon afterwards, João and Agostino split off with the knocker.

Felipe led the group farther down the corridor and stopped, as planned, around the corner from the control room. After half an hour, João and Agostino rejoined them, João giving them a thumbs up.

They waited, trying to rest, until the middle of the night cycle, when at least some pirates should be sleeping.

It was almost time. Annika checked her heater and longknife then went around the others, looking to make sure their heaters were turned to high. She tilted her head and tapped her helmet over her ear, indicating they should pay attention.

She put them into the formation they had drilled. After her, Felipe was front and center, with João and Tereza flanking him. Agostino and Madio were behind them, middle left and middle right, Isabel in the far back.

Then she gripped her heater in her left hand and drew her longknife with her right, feeling the hiss as the steel slid free from the sheath. The marinheiros drew their heaters.

Felipe entered codes into a panel. Lights blinked yellow. He thrust his head forward for a retina scan, and the first airlock door opened. They all crowded in. The lock began to cycle. Annika chanted to herself, "one-and-a-longknife, two-and-a-longknife, three-and-a-longknife, four-and-a-longknife, five-and-a-longknife..."

The second door opened, and they poured out, firing. Four faces jerked toward them. Looks of surprise and confusion. Playing cards flew up like birds and fluttered down. One man froze, holding a piece of food in his hand. Then they began to scramble for shelter, for weapons.

Annika dropped back. Felipe was a tiger—hot with anger and cold with self-control.

João was pointing his heater like a finger, firing calmly and accurately. A pirate tackled Madio, who reversed his grip on his heater and bashed in the man's face. Agostino was waving his heater around—it seemed only luck when he hit a pirate—but at least he wasn't hitting marinheiros.

One pirate stumbled out of the captain's cabin, holding a burner. He was too far away for the heater. Annika threw her longknife. "For the Norders! Pay in blood!" More people stumbled out of the captain's quarters, but they didn't seem to be armed.

Annika aimed her heater at a man reaching into a drawer. He leaped away as his hand blackened. She swept the heater back and forth. Pirates beat at charred and smoking clothing.

João holstered his weapon to help Isabel tangle some fallen pirates.

Tereza was being wrestled to the floor by a woman in a Norder tunic. Annika ran toward them. Now Tereza was on her knees, struggling, arms flailing. Annika pushed harder, but she was so far away, and her longknife was in a pirate's throat. Isabel charged in, jammed her heater in the Norder's face, and fired. The Norder jerked back, cursing. It was Liess.

Tears on her cheeks, Isabel was still firing, and Liess was crying out and beating at her scorched face. João wrapped a tanglecord around Liess, yanking it tight, and then took the heater away from Isabel.

Most of the pirates—there were 10 altogether, 11 including Liess— were lying on the floor, tangled, guarded by João and Madio. They had all suffered burns. Her own team seemed to be all right, except that Tereza was holding one arm stiffly, and Agostino was limping as he checked the captain's cabin for pirates.

Cords wrapped around the wire mesh covering the pilot's body and fastened her to her seat. Her eyes were closed but moving back and forth under her lids. Her head kept swaying, her hands paddling aimlessly.

They had won. Annika puffed out a breath and pulled off her helmet. Huh. She and the marinheiros had won.

Annika kicked Liess in the side. "You betrayed the ship. The Norders. The marinheiros."

Liess stared at the floor, hissing with pain, burned face twitching. Another kick. Liess glared up, lips pulled back from her teeth. "You have no idea how people look down on us. Living in barracks. Eating in dining halls. Hardly anything of our own. Last year when I was at Belle Reine, I was Blood Ring champion, but they laughed behind their hands at me, as I went on stage to accept an award in my one dress tunic with the mended rip. The pirates offered money. I did it for the money. Luiz helped me. She pointed with her chin at her tall marinheiro friend, lying on the deck a few feet away, then turned her face away from Annika.

Annika didn't know what to feel. Disgust. Rage. But also pity?

"Felipe da Silva V, Third Mate." Felipe was leaning over the control console for another retina scan. "I am the highest-ranking officer in the control room."

The ship's computer replied in its calm, pleasant voice, "Third Mate Felipe da Silva V, acknowledged."

"Sound the all-clear. *Enquanto la vida, há esperança.*"

Tereza had strolled over next to Annika. "Where there's life, there's hope."

Annika nodded. Since she was going to be working for the marinheiros, she should learn the language.

Annika stood in the communications center tossing a message cube from one hand to the other. She and her father had had some communications back and forth. It was hard having to record herself, wait for her father to respond, then explain herself again.

He'd invited her to join him on Elumet 8. When she had told him she'd be training marinheiros, he didn't seem to understand. "You're training ship's crew? Are they going to be soldiers?"

"No, no, no." She'd tried to put it simply and plainly. "Training them to defend the ship."

"I can get you a job here."

She had just finished recording her latest video. "No, I like it. I want to stay. I'm going to stay." She dropped the message cube into the transmission queue.

The coffee girl came in with a tray of heavy white cups, Madio's ring gleaming on her finger. Annika reached out and grabbed a coffee.

"Bom dia," said Annika.

"Bom dia."

Where Do You Keep Your Secrets?

In a metal box
locked with a key which you have melted
    in the fireplace,
painted with hexes,
double-wrapped with wire-core rope
    around lid and hinge and base,
and drowned in the river.

You gnaw your fingers
in dread that the box has been found
and cracked open with a rock.

The secrets tumble out
and quicktail it home—
to drop their guano on the lawn,
roost in the trees,
and screech from the eaves.
Each cry whittles you littler.

You totter down the basement steps,
bolt the door behind you.
Odors of mold and spider nests.

Jars on a shelf, peppers, tomatoes, okra
floating shadowy in brine.
You pry up a paraffin lid.
One leg, then the other—
you climb in.

Ako

Ako was bored. He was rich, and he had done almost everything a man could do. Had travelled up and down the Mother River beneath a triangular white sail, trading amulets for spices and selling the spices for a good profit. But it became work, and the work tiresome. Had lain with women of exquisite beauty and one of surpassing ugliness, who had given the most pleasure of all. Had tried hashish, but it only soothed him when he craved excitement. Had raced specially bred camels against his friends, thunder boiling and lightning cracking all around. Had lost all of his camels in a game of chance, and that had twisted his heart a little. The next day, bored, he'd won them back. Had faced a lion holding only a shield and a heavy iron-tipped spear, his body shuddering with fear and excitement. A month later he'd done it again, but he didn't get the same thrill.

And so the thought crept into his mind that he might kill a man. Any man. He found himself choosing a possible victim, planning the attack, devising the perfect way to kill him. Drown him in the river? Crack the eggshell bones in his throat? Punch through the chest with a lion spear? Then he began imagining how to get away with it; part of the thrill would come from evading detection, from outwitting the enforcers and fooling everyone else. He pictured himself with friends, discussing who could have been the murderer.

The idea invaded his mind more and more frequently. He couldn't talk to someone without deciding where to turn the knife. Or how he would knock him unconscious and shove him into the brick-drying kiln. Or feed him poison and watch froth bubble onto his lips. He began to wonder if he should do it just to free himself of the obsession.

He didn't view himself as a bad man. It was just that all the juice seemed to be squeezed out of him. Food had no flavor. He had no desire for women. He would take his favorite horse out for a ride and return in a few minutes. He couldn't bear to be in company but jumped up, complaining about the conversation, the musicians, the color of the walls. His friends laughed and said he had been bitten by the jumping bug. And he smiled and thought how he would kill them.

Then he started thinking about killing a woman. How he might reach around her from behind and curl his hands around her neck, pressing the sweet spot in the throat. How the soft body would jerk in his arms.

He went to a priest but talked in such a roundabout manner that the priest couldn't make sense of what he was saying. As the priest probed with question after question, Ako answered more and more vaguely. At last the priest, irritated, said Ako should visit his ancestors and pray for guidance. Then he paused, and with a sympathetic look said, "Your parents are dead, I think? You lost them at a young age?"

"My mother when I was 10 years old. My father a few years later." His mother had died in childbirth, and his baby sister two days afterwards. He had finished carving the wooden toy he was making for her and placed it in the tiny box with her remains. After the deaths his father had been kind to him, had allowed him to go out and return whenever he pleased, had given him money whenever he asked—but had rarely smiled or laughed. Ako knew he died of a broken heart.

It had been quite a while since Ako had visited the City of the Dead—three years? more?—but it didn't seem to have changed. The gatekeeper stood at the gate, hood pulled down over his face. The honeywoman chirped, "Honeybread? Honeybread?" selling sticky rolls from her basket.

Ako still remembered the way to his ancestors' restinghouse and strolled down the gravel path. Families were coming and going, men in colorful cloaks, women in all their jewelry, children in clean clothing with combed hair. A sundog trotted by at a distance, a child running after it. "Here, sundog! Here! Here!" The sundogs were always there, and the children always wanted to pet them, but hardly anyone ever did. When he was a child, he had cried and asked his parents to buy him a sundog, but they told him it was one thing money couldn't buy.

The path led through a belt of trees and came out at a rise in the ground, where it stopped at the restinghouse. Tiny flecks of mica in the imported stone glinted in the sun. Standing in front of the house, hands clasped in front of her, was the Memory Speaker he had hired. She was Remembering the ancestors neither too quickly nor too slowly. Some speakers rushed through the chants, wanting to finish and get on to the next commission, but this woman gave each word weight and meaning.

She saw him and nodded but continued with the chants. She had come to his great-grandmother. "Panya was as timid as a mouse, except when it came to her children. Then she had the heart of a lion and the cunning of a jackal." Ako noticed the Memory Speaker had streaks of gray in her hair that he didn't recall seeing when he had interviewed her, but he had paid very little attention to her looks. His elderly cousin who used to chant the memories had died, and it had fallen to him to either do the Remembering himself or hire a Memory Speaker. Although he talked to several who were interested in the commission, he liked the questions this one asked, showing a personal interest in his ancestors.

Now she had come to his little sister. "Baby Masika, born during the rain, who never cried, couldn't bear to be separated from her mother, and followed her into death's river." The Memory Speaker ended and stood quietly for a moment, giving the dead the contemplation that was their due.

Ako wondered what would be Remembered about him, and who would chant it.

The Memory Speaker turned to him. "I hope you like my chanting. Did you come today to listen?"

"No, I wasn't planning—I wasn't thinking—"

She said, "Were you planning to chant the memories yourself? Sometimes people want to do it to save themselves my fee for the day."

Her demeanor was so serious. He wondered if she ever smiled. "I'm afraid I came here without really thinking about it. Without thinking it through, I mean." He didn't know what he meant.

She said, "If you prefer doing the chants yourself, I'll refund today's cost." Her hand went to the bag at her waist.

He put his hand on her wrist. "No. You did the chants. You did them well. I probably couldn't even remember them."

"Thank you."

Her hand let go of the bag, and Ako let her wrist slide out of his grasp, although he wanted to hang onto it as onto a safety line. "You did them beautifully."

There was silence. He found himself looking at her mouth, which had formed the chants, at the curve and plumpness of the lower lip. The lips parted.

"I have two more commissions today. But I'm glad you came. I've been wanting to thank you for your payments. I appreciate that they come so promptly, and in advance."

"Don't thank me. My secretary sees to things like that."

"But the orders come from you." She smiled, the middle of her mouth puckering as if for a kiss, while the corners stretched. He wanted to see her smile again. But she was leaving, walking gently down the gravel path.

He realized he had not thought about killing her. He knelt and prayed, and hoped the obsession was gone.

Several days went by, and he felt light and happy. On the next feast day he and some friends went to a tavern. At a very late hour, the only ones left, they were pushed out by a yawning owner. One by one they staggered to their beds, except for Ako and his last remaining friend. They propped themselves against each other singing "Down to the Mother River." It seemed only natural to take the path to the water. Ako could push his friend's head under. Hold it there as air from the lungs bubbled to the surface. The body would twist and fight. Until finally it relaxed, went still. His friend mumbled something and bent over to be sick. Ako stopped. Then forced his body to turn around. Willed his feet to walk away. To take him home.

The next day Ako didn't wake until afternoon. His servant came in with food. What if Ako looped the cotton napkin around the man's scrawny neck and pulled? The eyes bulging, the face turning purple.

He grabbed whatever clothing lay on top of the chest and raced to the City of the Dead. He hurried to the restinghouse, looking for the Memory Speaker. She wasn't there. He thought back. It had been Sun's day when he saw her. She wouldn't be coming back until tomorrow. But perhaps she was chanting in another part of the City. Even though he

knew it was hopeless—there were hundreds of restinghouses—he
wandered down the paths looking for her as the sun drifted lower and
shadows stretched longer. A child was playing alone in a distant corner,
no one near, no one in sight but a sundog lying on its belly. Ako could
approach the boy quietly and lift him off his feet and bash his head
against a stone. A watery thunk. The sundog rose to its feet, eyes pinned
on Ako. It took a stiff-legged step toward him, growling.

Ako returned to his ancestors' restinghouse. This time when he
prayed, he took the posture of supplication, prone on the ground, face to
the earth, hands reaching out to the sides. He didn't hear the first bell
warning that the gates would soon be closing. He didn't hear the deep-
voiced bell calling all stragglers to come now, now, now. Didn't hear the
gate closing.

When he had finished praying and got up to go home, the grass was
damp. It was twilight; the traveler's star was high above the trees, and the
sun's pale sister rising. When he came to the gate, he saw it was closed
and locked. He shook the bars and called, but the gatekeeper didn't show
himself. There was no other exit.

Not knowing what else to do, he sat down on the grass, leaning back
against the cold iron of the gate, pulling his cloak around himself.

A pack of sundogs poured out of the trees, racing toward him. They
surrounded him, and he wondered if they were going to tear him apart.
It would be what he deserved. It would be what had to happen, to stop
him from killing. He hoped death would come quickly. But they wagged
their tails and thrust their cold noses into his neck and licked his face. He
couldn't move from astonishment. When they finished greeting him,
they lay down around him in a circle, one even sprawling heavily across
his knees. The dog's body and breath were warm. As the moon made her
silent way across the sky, his tense muscles loosened, and he drifted into
dreams.

In the morning, when the gatekeeper went to unlock the gates, he
saw that there was a new sundog, its eyes blinking against the light.
When the pack got up and stretched, the new one rose clumsily, as if it

were unaccustomed to four legs. The others trotted away, and the new one lurched after them.

Later that day the Memory Speaker came to Ako's ancestral restinghouse and chanted the Memories. While she was standing in contemplation, a muzzle was thrust into her hand. She caught her breath. Barely moving her head, she looked down and saw a sundog. "Oh you beautiful thing," she whispered. She slid her hand down the silky fur on the face and through the rich, dense fur around the neck. The sundog licked her wrist and lay down at her feet.

Later she heard that Ako had disappeared. She went to his secretary, who told her to finish the month she had been paid for and then stop. She followed his instructions. But she wondered what had happened to Ako. He had seemed so generous, so kind, with no condescension, that one time he had visited.

Even after the month's obligation had passed, she visited the restinghouse every week to chant her Memory of him. Often a sundog lay in the trees nearby, head up, ears flicked forward, seeming to listen.

A Coin for the Ferryman

I think it is the end
but it opens.
I think it is my own blood
but it is a river of light.
I think it is a bird
but it is a boat.
I think it is a shadow
but it is the ferryman.

When I come to the landing
I explain that I left swiftly, without warning,
and did not bring a coin.
He says he will accept a poem.
So I stand at the bow
as the boat pulls away
and speak the truest words I know.

Those might be drops of river spray;
those might be tears he wipes away.

Acknowledgements

Several stories and poems in this volume have previously appeared, sometimes in different versions, in online and print journals. My thanks go to the editors of the following publications: *Bards and Sages* ("The fa Liri Line"); *Daily Science Fiction* ("Wider and Deeper"); *Fictitious Force* ("Festival"); *Litbop* ("At the River"); *Mythic Delirium* ("Crow Eats Carrion" and "The Woman Who Lived by the Ocean Was Lonely and Tried to Make Herself a Husband"); *Talebones* ("God as a Swarm of Bees"); *Tales of the Talisman* ("Visitation," "The Hunt," "Honeybread," "Sacrifice," "Ako," and "A Coin for the Ferryman"); *Trapeze Magazine* ("one doll missing").

I want to give a huge thank you to fabulous, out-of-this-world editors Snežana Žabić and RD Morgan for their trust in me and for their sharp eyes.

My writing critique group always makes my work better. Much gratitude is due them, including Enid, who is in the next world, but whose words still resonate in my head.

Grateful thanks to guide stars Debra, Don, Elyssa, Ginger, Kate, Mary, Monica, and Scottie, to teachers Con Hilberry and Colette Inez, and to others, too many to list here.

And love to my husband, Gene, with gratitude for his support all these years.

About the Author

Carma Lynn Park is a Chicago-based writer, poet, and photographer. Her mother passed on a love of writing, and her father gave her a taste for fantasy and science fiction. She fondly remembers sitting on the cold linoleum floor of the back porch surrounded by cardboard boxes of fantasy and science fiction magazines.

You can read more of Carma's poems and see some of her photographs on her website, carmalynnpark.com.

www.ingramcontent.com/pod-product-compliance
Lightning Source LLC
Chambersburg PA
CBHW050030040726
47599CB00015B/1612